RIMROCK RIDER

Center Point
Large Print

Also by Walker A. Tompkins and available from Center Point Large Print:

Bushwack Bullets
Texas Renegade

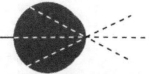

**This Large Print Book carries the
Seal of Approval of N.A.V.H.**

RIMROCK RIDER

Walker A. Tompkins

CENTER POINT LARGE PRINT
THORNDIKE, MAINE

This Center Point Large Print edition
is published in the year 2023 by arrangement with
Golden West Inc.

First US edition: Macrae Smith Company

The text of this Large Print edition is unabridged.
In other aspects, this book may vary
from the original edition.
Printed in the United States of America
on permanent paper sourced using
environmentally responsible foresting methods.
Set in 16-point Times New Roman type.

ISBN 978-1-63808-870-7 (hardcover)
ISBN 978-1-63808-874-5 (paperback)

The Library of Congress has cataloged this record
under Library of Congress Control Number: 2023938632

For
DUNCAN P. JACKSON

RIMROCK RIDER

Cast of Characters

BUCK TEMPLE: Bullets don't scare a man so much when he's been in the shadow of the noose.

JORD RAMONT: He wasn't going to let a few small ranchers keep him from a fortune in timber.

AVIS MALLOY: She'd once worn Buck's ring, but then she figured a girl has to look out for herself.

MARY WUNDERLING: She lived alone in the valley forest because she preferred nature's peace to man-made brawls.

KARL GOTHE: Always a sharp trader, he didn't hesitate to swear away another man's life if it meant closing a good bargain.

JOHN BROCKWAY: Sheriff of Rimrock, he stood by the word of the law even if it meant going after a friend.

JINGO PALOO: Mountain mail rider with a special delivery message for a condemned man.

Chapter 1

Standing at the narrow barred window of the death house cell, Buck Temple avoided looking at the sinister shape of the penitentiary gallows below, with the new yellow hang rope waiting to snap him into eternity with tomorrow's dawn.

The mark of the cattle range he would never see again was on this man, in the oiled bronze tone which weather had put on his face, in the solid muscle of his deep chest and the leather-lean shape of his arms. His eyes were the eyes of a man used to endless distances; therefore, he savored hungrily the flaming beauty of this last sunset.

Beyond the gun-turreted ramparts of the Territorial prison, he had a restricted, wholly precious view of lonesome hills rearing their rounded shoulders to a frosty sky. Heralding the approach of spring, patches of chocolate-brown earth were beginning to show piebald against the melting snows which marbled that cattle range, rolling off and away toward the Blue Mountains and Oregon.

He thought of Avis Malloy's eyes when the first stars pricked their diamond points through the arching blue, and her remembered loveliness softened the bleak line of his mouth, bringing brief forgetfulness of the grim events which had brought him here.

In the adjoining cell the Skidrow Kid whined a complaint. "What comfort can a man git sizin' up the noose that's goin' to cut off his wind? Pass along the makings, Buck."

Temple turned reluctantly from the window, showing a sympathy which the Kid in no way deserved. This sniveling dope fiend had slit the throat of a Chinese opium peddler. He was scheduled to mount the thirteen steps tomorrow immediately behind Temple.

Through the clotted gloom the wharf rat appraised Temple with a morbid admiration showing in red-rimmed eyes that were raw and drained dry by days and nights of weeping. This cowman, convicted of shooting a man in a rangeland ambush, had shown no slight sign of cracking under the strain of this interminable wait in Condemned Row. Something in Temple's steely insouciance shamed the Skidrow Kid, angered him by its contrast to his own craven wretchedness.

The match which Buck Temple now touched to his cigarette lit up the rugged planes of his face, accentuating the thrust of bronzed jaw and cheekbones, the crowfoot spray of wrinkles fanning out from either eye. At twenty-nine this man's thick and unruly hair was too black to show the bleach of a lifetime's suns and rains and winds. The big rope-calloused fingers holding the match were rock-steady, unlike the mounting palsy which haunted the Skidrow Kid.

"Why, a man sees what he wants to see, Kid," Temple said softly passing his Durham and papers through the bars. "I was looking at those hills out yonder. Wishing I had my blue stallion under me for just one hour and the wind on my cheeks again, riding those hills. But you've never rode, you said. You've missed the best part of life, Kid, skulking in your city slums."

The Skidrow Kid was unimpressed. "I'm a hophead who cut a Chink's throat in a waterfront alley; you shot your man out in the wide open spaces. What's the difference? We both wind up sucking the same dry bottle."

Temple said, "A man can't control the length of his life, Kid, but he can shape the depth and the breadth of it. I'll sack my saddle tomorrow with nothing on my conscience. Will you?"

The simple philosophy of this rider penetrated the Skidrow Kid's shell of arrogant contempt for decent things. He said, "You claim you didn't kill that man. Mebbe that's why you ain't caved so far. But when the warden cuts off your light with that little black cap tomorrow—you'll crack then, my bucko."

The Kid chuckled thinly, as if he found comfort in his taunt. His pallid, unwholesome face was a chalky oval in the gloom of the death house as he licked his cigarette.

"Funny, come to think of it," the Kid continued.

"You bein' the first man to hang since they built this pen. And you claimin' you are innocent. But, hell, we all claim that—even me."

Buck Temple lay down on his cot, stretching out long legs that carried the warp put there by twenty-odd years in saddle. He seemed wholly at ease, and he was; a man couldn't be bluffing, this close to the end.

"How'd you git into this jam, Buck?"

The Skidrow Kid had heard the gossip about this big rider, but he wanted to talk; for only in talk could he find surcease from the acid of despair that was fast eroding his own sanity.

The pink coal in the end of Temple's cigarette ebbed and glowed as the cowman sent his tobacco smoke into the tug of wind currents drifting through the slotlike window above his cot.

"I had myself a cow spread this side of the Cascade Divide," Temple mused. "Broken Bit. Ran timber cattle, and leased summer range to the big outfits around Yakima and Ellensburg during the drought season. Then along comes this railroad building across the desert to salt water. That was the start of the trouble."

A wry bitterness deepened the creases which bracketed Temple's wide mouth, a deep unrest stirring his big frame.

"A railhead as close as Ellensburg would have saved us havin' to make long trail drives," Temple went on. "Only this railroad needed lumber for crossties and trestlework, and the nearest timber was on the hills above our ranches, the Rimrock country. A contractor named Jord Ramont showed up last fall, aiming to log the watershed us stockmen depend on to keep our graze from going back to desert. He had to be stopped."

Temple's voice trailed off; distance and memories of bitter things obscured his eyes, his mind traveling far away.

"So you shot a timber cruiser," the Kid prompted, drawing on his fund of gossip about this prisoner. "And now you're waitin' to join the poor bastard in hell."

Temple stirred irritably. "I didn't shoot him. There was a trader named Karl Gothe. Richest citizen in Rimrock, swung a lot of weight. He claimed in court that he was out elk-huntin' above my Broken Bit, saw me ambush Ramont's cruiser. They dug a .30-30 bullet out of the back of his head. Gothe swore it came from my Winchester. And so here I am."

The Kid made an obscene clucking sound, enjoying this.

"If you'd had your druthers, you'd have killed Gothe and this Ramont before they brought you here, huh, Buck?"

There was a long run of silence before Temple answered that.

"I'd gun down Karl Gothe, anyway. At the time of the trial, I thought he'd made an honest mistake about that shooting. Since then, it's plain enough that Ramont was back of his perjurin' me. Last winter, he bought my ranch at sheriff's auction. Idea being he'll sell my timber to Ramont. And before Ramont is through he'll have ruined every rancher in those hills."

A key made its metallic rattle in the outer door. A premonitory shudder ran down the Kid's spine at the sound.

"Guard fetchin' our chow, Temple. Eat hearty. Take my rations if you want. I ain't been able to keep grub down."

A fanwise spread of lantern light cut the gloom of the twin cells as the iron door opened. But it was not the kitchen orderly wheeling in the last supper trays for these doomed men. Buck Temple recognized the blocky shape of Jeff Drumgriff, the warden of the penitentiary.

Drumgriff was grinning as he approached Temple's cell. He was carrying a sheaf of papers in one hand, lantern in the other.

Having been grilled time without number since the Rimrock sheriff had brought him across the desert to Drumgriff's custody, Temple averted his head now and said wearily, "After a last minute confession, Warden? You're wasting your time and mine. I've said my say. I'm playing it as it lies."

Warden Drumgriff unlocked Temple's cell.

"Nothing like that, son," he said gently. "This

paper is from the Governor's Mansion. It's not a reprieve. It's your release warrant. You won't sleep here tonight. You're free."

Buck Temple came to his feet, his six-foot stature dwarfing the corpulent official. The cowman's face was inscrutable in the lantern shine; his eyes searched Drumgriff, as if deciding whether this man was torturing him with hope where there could be no hope. Yet instinct assured him Drumgriff was no sadist.

"Here is a telegram from the sheriff in Rimrock," the warden's voice penetrated the confused swirl of Temple's thoughts. "It was delayed in transit due to a breakdown of the wires out of the Cascades. It arrived this evening, along with the Governor's release warrant. Thank God I received it in time."

Buck Temple accepted the yellow flimsy with an automaton's jerky movement, the words of message blurring together:

RIMROCK, W. T.
23 FEB 1887

JEFFERSON DRUMGRIFF ESQ.
WARDEN TERRITORIAL PRISON
WALLA WALLA W T

Vance Bluedom, a logger employed by Ramont Timber Company here, committed suicide this date after making written confession to murder of timber cruiser Lester McAllister last November 18, for which murder Buck Temple was sentenced to hang and remanded to your custody. Governor will contact you from Olympia. Letter follows. Please notify Temple immediately.

JOHN BROCKWAY, SHERIFF
CASCADE COUNTY, W T

The warden's pedantic jabbering sounded remotely distant and unreal in Buck's ears:

"I was almost the unwitting instrument of a ghastly miscarriage of justice. Let us return to my office."

Buck Temple pinched the cigarette stub hanging from his lips and flicked it through the grated window. The Skidrow Kid's face was pressed like a skull against the partitioning bars; it was the first time Temple had ever seen the Kid grin.

"Buck, good luck!"

He whispered, "Thanks, Kid." And followed the warden into the outer corridor.

This walk back to the administration building was like a fantastic sequence in a dream; it couldn't be happening to him. He found himself exchanging his prison dungarees for an ill-fitting suit of store clothes. Along with his release certificate, he received a crisp ten-dollar bill, society's largesse to all outgoing convicts of this institution.

The warden said unctuously, "One last bit of advice, son. I can readily understand the feelings you must be holding for this man Gothe, whose perjured testimony sent you to this place. You'll be going back to Rimrock, of course. I understand you have a girl waiting there—a girl you will marry. Don't jeopardize her happiness and your future by any desire to gain revenge, Temple."

Buck Temple grinned without mirth, "Avis Mallory." He spoke his fiancée's name as if it were a stranger's. "Warden, she never once wrote me during the months I been here. I wish she had. I'd feel better going back to her now."

Drumgriff, quick to note this man's evasion of Karl Gothe, went on earnestly, "Don't go running for the man who railroaded you this close to a noose, Buck. Let the law up there handle Gothe. Otherwise, I'll have this whole unpleasant routine to go through again—without this happy ending."

When the big gates of the brick quadrangle closed behind him, Temple moved uncertainly into the night, every sense whetted into a fine acuteness. Walla Walla's lights were like jewels clustered yonder in the black pocket of Mill

Creek's valley; the air was rank with the rich flavors of another spring.

He was as yet unable to realize he was free to walk down the road away from this place. After so many weeks of steeling himself psychologically for the noose, freedom was a sensation difficult to embrace.

He stood savoring the earthy smells of this night, the velvet touch of the wind on his cheeks; he was lost in the wonder of it when he saw a figure detach itself from the deep gloom of the penitentiary wall and call him tentatively by name.

Temple called back, "Jingo Paloo?" A wash of gladness springing through him as he recognized the Texas accents of the pony-mail courier whose circuit included his Broken Bit ranch.

"Nobody else, son."

Their hands met, clasped; then Paloo's arms were around Buck's shoulders, emotion tugging at the throats of both of them in this moment of reunion. "I—I quit my run cold to make it over here to welcome you out, Buck. You had a close call. My God, I'm glad to see you, kid!"

Buck glanced around, believing he saw another figure in the roundabout gloom over by a poplar clump near at hand.

"You bring Avis with you?"

The mountain mail rider coughed. "Avis? She couldn't have left Rimrock if she—if old

Genesee would of let her, Buck. You got to understand, this was a bad winter on the east slope. Rimrock has been snowed in solid since November. You and the sheriff were the last men out o' Coppertooth Pass."

Temple felt the sharp needle of disappointment, along with a secret relief for what Jingo Paloo had hinted might be the reason why the girl had not paid him a visit here in Walla Walla. Old Genesee Malloy had never approved of his daughter's engagement to this small-tally cattleman; he had had ambitious plans for Avis from the moment she reached Rimrock as a schoolteacher four years previously.

"Let's head for town," Temple said, "and roust out some storekeeper. I won't feel right till I got a Stetson on my head and a pair of cowboots on my feet, with spurs on 'em. Spurs as big as potlids, Jingo. I couldn't show up in Rimrock in this getup."

They were heading down the penitentiary road toward the night-shrouded town. Paloo halted suddenly, grabbing his arm.

"Buck," Paloo swallowed. "Buck, you can't go back to Rimrock. That's why I played hooky from my mail run and skun acrost the Territory hell-for-leather to ride herd on you."

Temple's full attention was on Paloo; but he had a vague sensation that someone had followed them down the hill road. At the moment, Jingo's

21

words nullified the warning tocsin in the back of his head.

"I can't go back? The hell!" He seized Jingo's shoulders. "Why? Is it Avis? Has she busted our engagement? Don't you think I can understand how she could?"

Jingo Paloo's freckled, puckish face was full of misery.

"Well, not exactly Avis, Buck. Jord Ramont's been sparkin' her; no use hidin' that. But she was still wearin' your ring last time I was in Rimrock. That was Christmas Eve."

"If you ain't been in Rimrock since December, how'd you hear about McAllister's bushwhacker making his confession?"

Paloo laughed shakily, glad to steer the conversation away from personalities. They were resuming their walk down the long hillslope now, their feet sinking into the spring-thawed mire.

"You know how old Captain Collie flashes heliograph messages to Mary Wunderling, down at her homestead under Coppertooth Peak? I dropped by her place with my dog team. Collie had flashed her the news that the Gov'nor was turnin' you loose today."

Temple grinned, having trouble conjuring up any real memory of the girl Paloo had mentioned. "Mary Wunderling? That freckled little tike? Is she still holding down the fort alone?"

Paloo's voice was oddly strained as he said,

"Mary's nineteen now, Buck, and perty as they come. It's been five years since them Yakima bucks broke the reservation and scalped her people. But she's still hangin' and rattlin' on that homestead, game little thoroughbred she is."

They were nearing the outskirts of the cow town now, in sight of the kerosene flares marking the deadfalls and honkytonks beyond the railroad stock pens. Temple said, "Mary Wunderling means something to you, Jingo?"

Paloo, breaking into a jog trot to keep up with Temple's long strides, showed a flustered shyness. "I'd marry her tomorrow," the Texan admitted, "if I thought I had a chance."

Temple came to a halt in front of a livery stable's black archway, the smell of horses and leather and hay and manure exuding from that place compounding the sweetest perfume a range rider could know.

His thoughts backtracking, Temple mused, "So Jord Ramont is sweet on my girl, eh? We'll see how long he lasts when I get back in the whirl. After Gothe, Ramont is my meat."

Jingo Paloo said with unnecessary loudness, "Buck, you ain't goin' back to Rimrock! You got nothin' to go back to!"

Buck Temple caught the panic in his friend's voice. He said slowly, "I've got Broken Bit to go back to. How long do you think Karl Gothe will take to deed my ranch back to me after I give him a working over with a gun?"

Paloo shook his head desperately. "Gothe don't own Broken Bit no more, son. That—that's the bad news I hate to break to you. When Gothe heard you were on the loose, he unloaded Broken Bit to the one man who hates your guts, Buck."

This news rocked Temple more deeply than Paloo could know.

"Who'd he sell to? Ramont?"

"Worse than Ramont. You could handle him. Broken Bit belongs to Genesee Malloy now, Buck. He's already leased the timber on your range to Ramont. When it's logged off, your spread won't be worth a damn for graze."

Pure shock kept Buck Temple from speaking now. His home-coming was reduced to the return of a saddlebum, a prodigal. His intended father-in-law—a man who had pledged himself to break up Temple's romance with his daughter—was now in the saddle where Broken Bit was concerned. This was something he could not fight, without forfeiting the love of Avis Malloy.

"You got to understand how the deck's been stacked ag'in you, Buck," Paloo went on, pure misery in his voice. "Gothe's in the clear. Claimed he made an honest mistake, identifyin' you as McAllister's bushwhacker—and Gothe's too solid a citizen not to get by with it."

"Is Gothe solid enough to turn a bullet?"

"That's what I'm talkin' about, Buck. Gothe

24

and Malloy have Ramont's tough bunch backin' 'em now. They're expectin' you to come back on the prod. They'd have you ambushed the same hour you showed up in Rimrock. You can't go back!"

The mail courier's words came in an impassioned rush; they were cut short in this instant by the ear-slamming crack of a gunshot breaching the night's hush from somewhere behind them.

The bullet slapped Temple's cheek with the airwhip of its near passage, thudding into the livery stable at his shoulder.

His instinct of danger had been right. A gunslinger had trailed them down Penitentiary Road tonight. The death that Jingo Paloo said was waiting for him in Rimrock had crossed the Territory to cut him down in his first few minutes of freedom.

Chapter 2

Temple whirled and crouched in a purely reflexive motion, a ravening instinct to shoot back sending his hands to empty flanks where gun holsters were accustomed to ride.

He was in time to see the orange-purple flash of a following shot lace the black gut of an alley across the street, between a grain warehouse and a wheelwright's shop. Then both he and Paloo were dropping to the mud.

Jingo Paloo's gun answered that salvo, silenced it. Temple distinctly heard the slam of Jingo's slugs hammering human flesh. Bellied down in the muck of this street, they saw a man stagger out of the alley mouth, limning himself distinctly against the whitewashed wall of the warehouse.

The wiry little Texan at Buck's side lined his gun sights on that wounded man and drove in three more shots to finish the job.

The echoes of this brief spate of gunfire volleyed off across the town. As the sounds ebbed remotely into the far hills, Temple and Paloo crossed the street to reach the bullet-riddled shape sprawled alongside the warehouse.

Temple struck a match, cupping his fingers to hide its bloom of light, and had his quick look at the bloody, contorted face of the gunman who had trailed them down Penitentiary Road. In the following darkness Paloo spoke. "Stranger to me."

"Same here. A thug after the price of a drink, maybe. Every convict who leaves those gates carries a sawbuck."

Paloo grunted. "Don't josh me, kid. This was no accidental thing. Karl Gothe or Jord Ramont sent this *malo hombre* here to cut you out of the deck, keep you from showing up in Rimrock."

Temple laughed softly in the darkness, knowing the truth of Paloo's judgment. "This settles it, Jingo. I'll call Gothe face to face back in Rimrock. And Ramont as well. After this ambush try, nothing could keep me from going back."

Jingo Paloo sucked in a deep breath, knowing this thing had passed beyond his control now. Somewhere down the street they heard men shouting, roused by the shooting; a rider was galloping in their direction.

"We better get away from this dead one," the Texan said. "The quicker we leave Walla Walla the better."

Paloo's postal credentials were good for passage in the mail car of the Short Line train to Wallula. A Columbia River packet dropped them at Pasco next day, the jumping-off place for the remote settlements strung along the eastern footslopes of the Cascade Range.

It was from a window of the Wells Fargo stage-coach carrying them into the brooding immensity of the Washington wastelands that Temple got his first glimpse of the survey stakes marking the right-of-way of Pacific & Western's rails toward Puget Sound.

"There it comes, Jingo," Temple told his partner, gesturing at the passing landscape of sagebrush, the empty domain embraced by the Big Bend of the Columbia. "The railroad that will cost us foothill ranchers our graze if Ramont logs off the timber they'll need to build this line."

Paloo watched the passing grade markers with a morose eye. P & W's westering course was a preordained part of this frontier's destined growth; it would link the rich cattle and wheat country of Washington, the mines of Idaho and Montana, with salt water ports and a world-wide market.

Thrusting its steel across these treeless desert plains, Pacific & Western's direct need was lumber for crossties and trestles, wood to fuel its locomotives, wood to bridge the mighty Columbia and shore up its Cascade tunnels.

The nearest source of supply was the evergreen forests of the Cascades. This was the motive which had sent the Ramont Timber Company scouts swarming into the Rimrock country last fall, cruising for the nearest available logs.

"Why did Ramont have to pick on our Rimrock

slope?" Paloo asked sourly. "Knowin' that loggin' off them hills would ruin the watershed and leave you foothill ranchers open to havin' yore graze burnt out the first summer and your top soil washed to the ocean in the spring runoffs? Why don't he do his damned loggin' up in the Okanogan, say, where cattle ain't the mainstay of the people?"

Buck Temple, feeling the boredom of this jouncing trek toward the mountains just beginning to rear their snow-thimbled peaks on the northwest skyline, found welcome surcease in talk.

"It's a simple matter of man's greed, Jingo. Ramont would call it sound business tactics. He knows our timber is the closest to this new boom market. He can't haul lumber from as far off as the Okanogans and make a profit."

"But you cattlemen got some rights!"

"Ramont don't give a damn for ruining a few scatterin' timber-cattle ranches, let alone taking the summer graze away from the big Ellensburg and Yakima syndicates," Temple pointed out. "What does Ramont care if he turns the foothills back to desert inside of three-four years? The railroad will be built. Ramont will have his money."

Paloo, bracing himself against the giddy lurchings of the thoroughbraced Concord, shrugged pessimistically.

"Try to tell that to the Territorial Legislature," he said. "Tell 'em that a string of two-bit cattle ranches are more important than havin' a new railroad cross Washington. This country has gone railroad crazy ever since the U P built into Californy, back in '69."

Temple eyed the passing drabness of the empty landscape, dourly admitting to himself the truth and weight of Paloo's argument. Ranchers like himself stood to sacrifice all they had built up through the years, to satisfy the greedy demands of a frontier railroad and ruthless timber contractor like Ramont.

"Spring thaws are openin' up the Rimrock country," Paloo went on. "Now that Genesee Malloy owns your range, there's nothin' to stop Jord Ramont from settin' up a sawmill on yore Broken Bit. When he's finished logging off your stand of timber in Glacier Canyon, what's to keep him from spreadin' out and ruinin' your neighbors? There ain't a bronc stomper in them hills with the guts to stand up to Ramont and his bunch."

There was no adequate rebuttal to that. As long as the other foothill cattlemen stood fast and refused to part with their timber rights to logging outfits like Ramont's, they had the territorial courts to look to for a decision that would save them from eventual ruin. But, as Paloo had hinted, there were ways and means for a determined and ruthless lumber outfit to put pressure on Buck Temple's neighbors. Now that Broken Bit was in the hands of a known enemy of the cattle interests, Ramont had his toehold in the hills. They had railroaded Buck Temple to the penitentiary in order to seize his Broken Bit; but even now that he had cheated the hang rope, he was returning to fight the cowmen's battle against unsurmountable odds.

"Ramont damn' near put me in boothill to get where he is this spring," Temple said bleakly. "I'll smoke that timber grabber to hell and back before I see him ruin our hills."

At Yakima, first town beyond the searing desert wastes of the Columbia Basin, Buck Temple got rid of his prison clothes and, using money borrowed from Jingo, showed up at the Mountain Express stage office wearing the more familiar habiliment of his calling.

A flat-crowned beaver Stetson of biscuit-tan color replaced his fedora. Waist Levi's were tucked into star boots, high of heel and fabricated of costly kangaroo leather, the product of the cow town's best cowboy bootmaker.

He had purchased a hickory workshirt, bandanna neckpiece and a blue ducking brushpopper jumper to cut the spring cold in the upper altitudes they were heading for.

Joining Paloo at the stage depot just as hostlers were hitching four Morgans to the Mountain

31

Express coach, Temple saw his friend's brows lift dubiously as he spotted the bulge of a gunstock at Temple's right hip.

Temple had purchased a Colt .45 single-action revolver, reposing in a cutaway holster of oak-tanned leather. The big brass-buckled shell belt which slanted across his midriff had a cartridge in every loop.

"You're as good as signin' yore death warrant, breezin' back to Rimrock with that hardware strapped to yore belly," Jingo Paloo voiced his blunt disapproval. "I've warned you that Gothe and Ramont have marked you for boothill bait as soon as you show up. I should 'a' got yore promise not to spend none of my loan on ammunition and hardware. Ain't there a law that prohibits a—"

Temple cut in sharply, a cold edge on his good humor.

"Now don't forget and make the slip of calling me an ex-convict, Jingo. I'm not even a parolee. The Governor didn't pardon me. I walked out of Walla Walla with no strings attached."

As the stage rolled up the valley on the first leg of its northward run to Ellensburg, Paloo said peevishly, "Well, there ought to be a law against any man carvin' another man's name on a bullet, which is what you're doin'. Karl Gothe, maybe Jord Ramont as well. All this'll get you is a chunk of ground in Rimrock's graveyard, Buck."

At Ellensburg a new driver took over the stage for the foothill run. Temple recognized this jehu as Billy Winn, one of Rimrock's old-timers, his friend since boyhood days.

Sitting aloof in the box, Winn put his rheumy eye on his passengers, shifted his quid to another corner of his cheek and said, "Good seein' you back, Buck."

Ten hours later, deep in the hills, Paloo left the stage at a relay station which was the headquarters of his mail route during the months that Rimrock town was snowbound. His parting admonition to Buck Temple was curt and cynical:

"I hope the thaws ain't opened Coppertooth Pass to you, Buck. You'll live that much longer. So long."

Buck Temple, riding the box with Billy Winn to escape the afternoon heat, was grateful for the old reinsman's ingrown silence, his complete indifference to his passenger's personal affairs.

Temple felt a boyish excitement growing in him when he got his first view of Coppertooth Peak, the thousand-foot fang of reddish lava rock which marked the beginning of the timber-cattle country, the landmark which outposted the Cascades and gave the Pass its name.

Day's end found Winn's coach at the foot of the slush-mired grade snaking up the Pass, ten miles short of Rimrock. As they came in sight of Grapevine Curve at the entrance to the Pass,

Temple spoke his first words to old Winn.

"Drop me off at Si Larbuck's cutoff, Billy."

The stage lumbered to a halt in the heavy gumbo where a side road snaked out of the thin timber. This was the margin of the jackpine country, delineating the mountain greenery from the desert blankness which comprised the eastern two-thirds of the Territory.

The wooded foothills lifted in thousand-foot terraces to meet the granite upthrust of the High Rim, topped by the lush Skyline Flats with the snow-white teeth of the Cascade Divide dominating this primitive scenery.

Descending from the mud-spattered stage, a homeward-bound prodigal without so much as a sacked saddle for baggage, Temple put his last words to the driver. "Don't mention me riding up with you when you hit town, Billy. When I left last fall I thought I wouldn't be back. So I gave my horse to Si Larbuck. I'd sort of like to ride into Rimrock forking my own leather."

The jehu said, "Sure, Buck, I ain't seen hide ner hair of ye." He kicked off his brake and sent his team toward the Grapevine, the stage soon swallowed up in the gathering dusk.

From the Pass road to Larbuck's little S Bar L ranch house on Greasy Grass Creek was two miles, uphill most of the way; it was full dark when Buck Temple knocked on Larbuck's door.

"Be gawd, and the bad penny has returned,"

Larbuck greeted him, masking his roused emotions behind a perfunctory handshake. A paternal grin lurked under Larbuck's gnarled beard as he ushered Buck into the aromatic warmth of his shack. "Been expectin' ye. You'll be wantin' that half-breed nag of yours back. Injun giver."

Temple inhaled the blended smells of hides and tobacco, boiling coffee and pineknot smoke with a keen sense of relish.

"Blue is half Morgan and half Quarter," he said with mock temper, "and much too good to carry you or your brand, Si."

Preliminary ribbing over, Larbuck dropped his air of spurious levity. Facing Temple across his supper-table, Larbuck said, "You've come back for a settlement with Karl Gothe?"

"Why, I aim to be reasonable with him. Give him his choice of leaving the country or staying permanent—six foot under."

Larbuck studied his guest with a calculating eye.

"You realize, o' course, that Gothe ain't the man you want. Ramont was back of your trouble. Gothe was his tool."

"Ramont's second on my list, Si. It's a case of getting him before he gets me, Paloo says."

Larbuck speared a venison steak, growling, "You realize the Foothill Cattlemen's Association has fell to pieces since you left last fall, Buck? Some of 'em are showin' signs of sellin' out their timber rights to Ramont?"

"Is it that bad, Si?"

"Worse. Ranchers on both sides of Broken Bit are swallerin' Ramont's fancy talk about how he can log off the government timber above their spreads anyhow, so they might as well string along with him and mop up some of the gravy."

Temple shoved back his chair and wiped his mouth with a bandanna. "Who of our neighbors are damn fool enough to grab at the immediate dollar and ruin their own future?"

"Well, Hal Dikus for one. Joe Redwine for another. After what happened to you, Buck, those bronc stompers are afraid to stand up to Ramont. That's what it boils down to."

Buck Temple grinned without mirth. "I want you to call a mass meeting of the Association here on your place for day after tomorrow, Si," he said. "We've got to whip the weak ones into line before Ramont digs in too deep."

Si Larbuck scanned his guest for a long moment, his eyes holding a heavy gravity.

"I've survived a range war or two in my time," he said, "in Wyoming and Texas. They're bad business. It'll take a solid front to freeze out Ramont. I ain't sure you can swing it, Buck."

Temple made a vague gesture. "This Rimrock slope has been cow country since my Dad's time, ever since men like you took it over from the Indians. It'll stay cow country." He got to his feet. "Got a hankering to see that roan of

36

mine and say howdy, Si. He out in the barn?"

Larbuck shook his head. "Tough winter, so I keep my stock up at the far end of Greasy Grass, where they got shelter and feed. Blue was fat and frisky last time I was up to the camp."

Buck Temple settled himself on the horsehide divan in front of Larbuck's fireplace and let his travel-sore muscles, soft after three months behind bars, soak up the welcome warmth. He knew that for him, leisure time to enjoy life this spring was an uncertain thing.

He was surprised to see Larbuck shrugging into a mackinaw and taking down a pair of snowshoes from a ceiling rack.

"I know you're anxious to git on to town and see Avis," the old man said, "and get along with your other affairs. So I'm goin' up the coulee after your pony tonight. Be back in time for you to hit Rimrock before noon tomorrow."

Mention of Avis Malloy put a faint bitterness in Temple's eyes.

"Avis has waited all winter," he said. "Another day won't make any difference, I reckon."

Shouldering the webbed footgear he would need to reach his destination tonight, Si Larbuck said from the doorway, "If this country is to be saved, Buck, you're the only man who can do it. It's a big order. If I didn't know you like I do, I'd tell you you are a plain fool for showing up in Rimrock again."

Heading off into the darkness toward the maw of Greasy Grass Coulee, the old S Bar L boss's muttered introspection was picked up and blotted out by the night wind:

"Odds are a passel of men will die before this thing is over, with mebbe me at the top of the stack. And I got my doubts if Buck Temple will be around to see the dust settle. And him without a ranch of his own to fight for. Why are some men born to let another fight their battles?"

Chapter 3

A gathering blizzard, like a stinger on the end of winter's tail, brought premature dusk to Rimrock. This cow town's populace sought the comforts of its saloons, dreading the night ahead.

Inside the Mile-High Mercantile, trader Karl Gothe stationed himself at the window in his post office cubicle, beginning a vigil over the main street and the Coppertooth Pass road which linked this summit settlement with the outside world.

Gothe habitually closed his trading post at sundown and repaired to the Timberline Saloon for a session of poker and a friendly bottle. Tonight he passed up that routine to await the arrival of the year's first stage up from Ellensburg.

November through February, most years, Rimrock was sealed off from civilization by snow-blocked roads. The settlement depended on stored provisions to get through its winters, and on dog team sledges for its weekly mail.

A March Chinook had cleared the last high drifts off the Pass road, these last few days. Tonight should see the mail-bags arriving by stagecoach, providing Billy Winn's span of Morgans could negotiate the hub-deep gumbo and avalanche-scarred road.

For Karl Gothe, this first incoming traffic of the season held a deep menace. For the past week, the talk in Rimrock's honkytonks had centered on Buck Temple's escape from hang rope and the likelihood that Temple would be a passenger on the first stage to break the high country winter blockade. And if Rimrock knew Buck Temple, that puncher would come primed for a showdown with the man who had railroaded him to Walla Walla—Karl Gothe.

The corpulent trader, knowing the low esteem which this cattle town held for him since this past week's events had tumbled him off his pedestal of respectability, sensed the talk going on behind main street's false fronts.

Buck Temple had become a specter to haunt his sleep, ever since an obscure logger named Vance Bluedom had blown out his brains in a dingy back room of Straight-Edge Josie's bawdy house.

Bluedom, drunk though he had been at the time of his self-destruction, had left a message scrawled with a soft-nose bullet on the wall beside the bed where his corpse had been discovered by one of Josie's fancy girls.

That message named its writer as the real killer of timber cruiser Les McAllister at the head of Glacier Canyon, on Buck Temple's Broken Bit ranch, last November. That confession had been enough to release Buck Temple from prison.

Full dark had come to the cow town when Karl

Gothe, brushing the moisture off his windowpane with a sleeve, saw the twin lamps of the Ellensburg stage rounding the Pass road a mile to the east.

Gothe's square-jawed Teutonic face was oiled with cold perspiration as he checked the loads in the Remington .44 he carried naked under the girthband of his moleskin pants.

As he unlatched the door of his post office cubicle and waddled out into the store, a back door of the building opened and two men pushed in from the blackness of an alley.

They were Jord Ramont and his high-climber, Bull Corson; and Gothe knew without asking what had brought them so secretively into his mercantile store tonight.

"You figure Buck Temple will be on that stage that's pulling in, don't you, Karl?"

Ramont's voice carried a sharp edge, unlike the usual suavity Gothe was accustomed to hearing from this man whose personality had so muddied the current of Rimrock's life this past winter.

"Ja, dass ist so. Buck Temple comes to kill me, that I know."

Ramont had just ridden in from Broken Bit ranch, where his men were building a dam across Arrowhead Creek to make a holding pond for cut logs when the spring freshets came. He was in the wool shirt, corduroys, and steel-calked boots of any logger; but even in his rough garb, the man exuded authority and a ruthlessness capable of riding down any opposition.

His mouth was the dominant feature of a face women found striking; his teeth, showing now in a tolerant grin for Gothe's weakness, were vividly white under the close-cropped mustache which matched his close-cropped black hair.

By contrast, Bull Corson was a disreputable figure, his face Neanderthalic and scabrous with the marks of uncounted brawls.

"There will be no trouble," Ramont said, seeing the trader shift his six gun from his belt to a pocket of his mackinaw. "The sheriff is waiting out front. He expects Buck, too."

Gothe's pippin-red cheeks ballooned with his relief; he was savoring what amounted to a reprieve from a death sentence.

"Get out there and meet the stage as if nothing was wrong," Ramont growled, walking over to a pot-belly stove and lifting numb hands to its cherry-pink sides. "Brockway will handle Temple."

"Ja. I am vantin' no troubles, Yord."

Opening the street door, Gothe saw Sheriff Canuck Brockway leaning against a porch post, as Billy Winn braked the Ellensburg stage to a halt. Winn was already untying the tarp which shielded Rimrock's mailbags from the weather. The Concord's window curtains were down, concealing any passengers who might be aboard.

Deep in his pocket, Gothe's hand clamped over his gun butt.

Sheriff Brockway, sheepskin collar turned up against the night's chill, stalked down the Mercantile steps as the stage tooler tossed four bulging mailsacks over the railing.

"Any passengers with you, Billy?"

Karl Gothe held a sucked-in breath until he caught old Winn's grunted answer. "Not this run, Sheriff. Folks down below didn't think I could make it. I'll be full up next week."

Billy Winn kicked off his brake and picked up his ribbons, lashing his jaded Morgans on downstreet to where a small crowd had gathered at the Mountain Express depot to applaud the arrival of this wheeled harbinger of spring.

Canuck Brockway, standing there on the plank sidewalk, turned to watch Karl Gothe shoulder the heavy mailsacks, and the lawman's clipped drawl came sarcastically through the dark:

"Buck's given you another week to sweat, Karl."

Ignoring the jibe, Karl Gothe dragged his mailsacks inside the store and turned to meet Jord Ramont's inquiring glance. The big German was trembling visibly, as the reaction of his week-long suspense drained out of his nerves.

"Temple wasn't aboard, I see."

Gothe's temper, rubbed raw by the lumberman's bantering voice, broke its shackles now.

The big trader lumbered forward, fingers coiled around the butt of his Remington deep in his pocket.

"Yord, I vant my money. I am vantin' it now, py Gott. I am goin' to leaf dis *verdamdt* town. For me iss nozzings left."

Jord Ramont's deep-socketed eyes held a glittering sheen of contempt for the big German as he stared back at Gothe.

"Our agreement," he reminded Gothe in a soft voice, "was contingent upon established proof of Buck Temple's death. Your perjury in court didn't pay off, my friend. You promised to get Temple out of the picture. So far he is still a threat. As long as he is, you get no money from me."

Gothe's vast lungs heaved to the stridor of his breathing. Fear and anger and a consuming hatred for this suave newcomer to Rimrock put their fire in the trader's yellow eyes now.

"Nein! I vant my money. Iss it my fault that Bluedom kilt himself? You are lucky he did not betray all of us before he blew oudt his pig brains, Yord."

Jord Ramont came to his feet with a catlike swiftness, reaching out to lock a hand on the arm Gothe kept rammed in his mackinaw pocket, clutching the gun there.

"Get back to your mail sorting, you swine, and keep that gun in your pocket."

44

Karl Gothe broke free of Ramont's grip and turned back to his mailbags. Jord Ramont plucked a cigar from his shirt pocket and stuck it between his teeth, measuring the big German with a careful eye as Gothe plodded back to his post office cubicle.

Then, turning, Ramont motioned for Bull Corson to follow him as he unbolted the trading post door. Out on the porch, Ramont paused to light up his cigar.

"Karl Gothe is a dangerous man," Ramont said to Corson, as they headed down the steps. "Any pressure from Temple and he might spill his guts. I think I will have to kill Gothe."

Corson said throatily, "You say the word, boss, and—"

Ramont shook his head. "I'll handle this myself, Bull. Maybe Gothe will skip town before Temple shows up."

Corson grunted. "The mistake was made last fall, boss. You should have let me smoke Temple out of the picture."

Ramont eyed his hulking woods foreman with a tolerant grin.

"Leave the thinking to me, Bull. Bushwhacking Temple would have whipped these foothills ranchers into line to fight us to the last ditch. We had to use a local citizen to break Temple. Gothe served his purpose. As he said, how could we foresee Bluedom's confession?"

· · ·

Inside the Mile-High, Gothe took the better part
of an hour to sort the incoming mail. A crowd had
gathered on the Mercantile porch before he was
half finished, shaking the locked door at frequent
intervals, impatient to pick up their mail.

When Gothe finally opened the store to admit
the throng, old Captain Collie, Rimrock's lowliest
citizen, was the first to squirm past him into the
store. A veteran of Civil War campaigns, Collie
was spending his sunset years drinking himself
to death in this cow town, supported by his
soldier's pension. As a Union signalman, Collie
had never gained a rank beyond that of corporal;
the captain's tunic he wore, the tarnished battle
medals which he flaunted, had had their source in
some pawnshop.

Scuttling to the head of the line forming at
the post office wicket, Captain Collie's liquor-
thickened voice carried to every person in the
line:

"You figgered Buck Temple would be on that
stage tonight, eh, my friend? Haw! There'll be a
new postmaster in this burg after Buck does show
up. Eh, Karl?"

Laughter greeted the old pensioner's jibe; Karl
Gothe's thick, corded neck took on a brick-red
hue as he thrust a government pension envelope
through the window, the only mail Collie had
ever been known to receive.

46

"Take your charity undt git oudt uff my store, you drunken swine!" snarled the trader. "Who iss next?"

Captain Collie thrust his envelope into a pocket of his faded army tunic and shuffled off into the shadowy confines of the store, gibbering gleefully.

The old derelict was not the only man to rub salt in Gothe's tender wounds. Texas Sam Waterby, who ran timber cattle beyond the ridges north of Temple's Broken Bit, accepted his mail and had his advice for the postmaster:

"Don't get the idea Buck won't be coming back just because he missed the first stage, Karl. I was in your boots, I'd try to talk Genesee Malloy into letting Buck have Broken Bit back. You made a mistake, selling out to Malloy."

When Gothe had finished passing out mail and had bolted the door on his last patron, the trader felt a condemned man's withering strain.

Outside, a high cold wind was beginning to lash Rimrock's roofs; the ache in Gothe's joints told him that the settlement was in for another blizzard before winter retreated beyond the high peaks.

The fat trader stared at the blazing windows of the Timberline Saloon across the street, and felt a moment's intense yearning to enjoy the comfort of a glass of whisky there. But he knew what the men lining the Timberline bar would be talking about. Buck Temple. Why hadn't Buck Temple been aboard that stage tonight? What was delaying his inevitable return?

Feeling the blast of the coming storm shivering the log walls of his establishment, Gothe went outside and made the rounds of his windows, closing and latching the big plank shutters, so recently opened after winter's long siege.

Coming back to his front door, Gothe brushed an accumulation of mealy snowflakes off his shoulders, stamped mud and snow from his hobbed boots. This blizzard would be a heller.

He saw a man step out of the Trail House Hotel, directly opposite the Mercantile, bundled in an oilskin slicker, but Gothe knew it was Jord Ramont, and an unreasoning hatred, mixed with fear, coursed through the trader.

Ramont's slicker-shrouded figure was swallowed up in the darkness across the street; Gothe wondered what sent the lumber boss abroad in this snowstorm, away from the comfort of his suite of rooms in the hotel.

Something akin to terror made Gothe hurry the job of unlocking the door and retreating into the shelter of his store. For the first time, Gothe realized the full crushing weight of events shaping up against him, touched off by Buck Temple's unpredictable escape from hang rope doom.

Next to Temple, Gothe knew that Jord Ramont

was the man most likely to destroy him. Knowing the depths of Ramont's ruthless nature, Gothe felt a numbing prescience that he had been unwise in pressing the lumberman for his Judas pay tonight.

Gothe made the rounds of his lamps, blowing each one out until he came to the one above the counter where he kept his brandy cask. Feeling the need of a drink, Gothe fumbled on a shelf for a snifter glass and drew a stiff jolt of liquor.

He was cupping the globular glass between his shaking palms when he caught sight of a human shape sprawled asleep in the runway behind his counter. It was Captain Collie, the odor of pilfered brandy strong on the old sot's stringy whiskers.

Mouthing Teutonic profanity, Gothe seized the drunken oldster by his galluses and dragged him from behind the counter. A savage kick to the short ribs made the old derelict squirm with pain, his eyes flickering open.

Gothe grabbed the man by the ankles and dragged him across the floor like a sacked dog. Opening the street door, the trader yanked Collie across the porch. A rib-cracking kick rolled him out into the muddy gutter beside the plank sidewalk, moaning feebly.

Karl Gothe stalked down the steps, a beast's fury in him as he lifted a boot with the intention of stamping the iron hobnails again and again into Collie's face. But a voice out of the night arrested him as he stood with up-poised knee:

"That's enough, Karl."

The trader froze, knowing that voice; then he whirled to stare at the slicker-clad shape which was taking form just beyond the bar of lamplight spilling through the doorway.

Gothe yelled, "Temple, damn you!" and pulled his gun.

He whipped up the barrel, firing point-blank in blind panic. The gun's heavy concussion was immediately swallowed up by the storm's roar down the channel of the street's false fronts.

Incredibly, his target did not fall. Gothe eared back his gunhammer for a second shot, when the man made his own draw and flame spat its nozzle jet from a Colt's bore.

The bullet took Gothe between the eyes. It knocked his elephantine bulk off balance. Falling, the dead man rolled soddenly off the steps to half cover Captain Collie in the mud. Before the old derelict could extricate himself, Gothe's killer had vanished behind the swirling snow-flakes.

Five minutes later Collie was facing Sheriff Brockway in the jail office of the courthouse building. The tower clock was sounding the stroke of twelve midnight as Collie faced the old lawman.

"Sheriff, you got a dead one to pick up. Front

of the Mile-High. Karl Gothe. Good riddance to the town."

Brockway sighed, reaching for his ring of keys, aiming to let Collie sober up overnight in his cell. He was long accustomed to this derelict's wild fabrications when he came in off a binge.

"By gawd, it's the truth!" protested Collie. "I seen the shootin', didn't I? Gothe fell acrost my laigs, didn't he? Time I wiggled out from under the Heinie, his killer had vanished like a cloud o' smoke."

Brockway studied Collie with patient attention.

"All right, Cap. Who shot Gothe? If he's shot?"

Cap'n Collie said, "Jord Ramont shot him— that's who."

Chapter 4

At Si Larbuck's place on the Greasy Grass, Buck Temple climbed out of his blankets at high noon of this sunless day to find the blizzard still raging and snow dunes piling against the weather side of the ranch house to window sill level.

He felt a moment's alarm, knowing that Larbuck was due back from his coulee camp long before now with the horses. Obsessed by a vague sense of worry over the old rancher's safety, Temple set about preparing a belated breakfast for two.

The kettle on Larbuck's rusty cookstove had boiled dry during the night and when Temple, shielded from the storm's blast by a buffalo coat of his host's, broke trail out to the pump, he found it frozen solid.

He melted snow in a tin wreckpan, got a good fire going in the mud-and-wattle hearth, and sliced a skilletful of sowbelly from Larbuck's well-stocked pantry. It was one o'clock when Temple had coffee boiling, and he knew then that he could never wait here. He would have to search for Larbuck.

This blizzard was one of those sneakers which built itself to striking strength on the west side of the Cascade Divide and then swooped across the Skyline Flats and the High Rim, with such devastating surprise that men caught away from shelter stood a fifty-fifty chance of freezing in some snowdrift.

Larbuck was past seventy, but tough as whang, a man who knew the myriad canyons and hogbacks of this range like the back of his own hand. Temple tried to comfort himself with the knowledge that the blizzard had not reached its height until after midnight; Larbuck had had a good seven hours to make his stock corrals at the box end of Greasy Grass, ten miles from the home ranch. The coulee was sheltered from these storms; stock fattened over the winter in the lee of its granite walls, so that Larbuck had never faced a winter die-off.

Strapping on a pair of Larbuck's, hickory-frame snowshoes, Buck Temple left the ranch house at two o'clock, packing a saddle pouch containing food and first aid supplies. The mouth of Greasy Grass was half a mile off, at the far rim of the grassy park which Larbuck had homesteaded fifteen years ago. Crossing this open area in the teeth of the blizzard would be the most dangerous part of his search.

Temple knew, from experience gained in his boyhood years, how easily a man could lose his bearings once familiar landmarks were lost behind the whorling white void.

It was a frailty of human and animal intellect

alike that, marooned in a blinding storm such as this one, they might circle endlessly until exhaustion brought the sweet comfort and synthetic warmth which presaged death by freezing—aimless spirals which might leave them to die within earshot of the point of their starting.

Locating Larbuck's drift fence which he remembered cut the open park in half, Temple bucked the drifts, keeping the barbwire guide at his left. Twenty feet from Larbuck's barn, he lost sight of the building. Snow was halfway to his knees on the level, with this storm only half a day old; drifts were already high enough in places to obliterate the five-foot posts which Temple was depending on to lead him to the coulee.

Alone in this lost white world, Temple's only sign of having left the meadow was when he felt the violent pressure of the snow-laden gale suddenly ease its strike against his back. Hemlock brush and wild rhododendron scrub whipped his buffalo coat, telling him that he was inside the coulee.

Common sense told him that the old-timer would hole up at his line-camp soddy rather than risk bucking the blizzard at night. But the fact remained that Larbuck was without grub; the Greasy Grass camp wasn't maintained during bad weather.

"Hell, he'd butcher a beef and settle down like a grizzly if this storm lasts out the day," Temple told himself. "It's not like this was the start of winter."

In the eerie half-light, Temple slogged on, his webs tangling with submerged brush and rocks every few yards. Larbuck, he knew, would make better time on snowshoes, since he was not handicapped by spike-heeled cowboots.

Then he came to a pocket of comparative quiet, where high bulwarks of Douglas fir broke the force of the storm sweeping over the coulee rims. There was more light here where the gulch widened; and Temple was halfway toward the closing avenue of conifers up-coulee when the wind brought to his ears a raveled shred of sound which he identified as a horse blowing snow out of his muzzle.

Temple halted, clumsy on his snowshoes, feeling the restrictive burden of the saddlebags, knowing then how tired he was, after so short a time. He keened the wind for a repetition of the sound; and then he saw the blurred shape of his own blue roan stallion breaking trail toward him.

At first glance, Temple believed Blue was alone, although it was not natural for the big mixed-blood to abandon a man, in the event accident or exhaustion had halted Si Larbuck.

He called Blue by name, and heard the big stallion's whicker of recognition run toward him on the wind. The Morgan-Quarter saddler brushed Buck Temple with an out-thrust muzzle as they met, one steel-shod hoof breaking the rawhide webbing of the man's left snowshoe.

He saw then that the stallion had a rope tied to its head-stall; and as his eye followed the sag of that rope off through the snow, he spotted Si Larbuck crunching slowly up the trail Blue had broken for him.

"You old mossyhorn, you had me spooked!" Temple complained, rounding the stallion and searching the old rancher's white-rimmed face anxiously. "You all right, Si?"

Larbuck spat a gobbet of steaming tobacco juice into the trailside drifts.

"All right? Hell's fire, o' course I'm all right."

Satisfied that the old rancher was in good shape, Temple turned to the blue roan with a stormy mixture of emotions seething through him. This time a short week ago, in the death house at Walla Walla, he had dreamed of this deep-brisketed animal as some men might dream of a woman forever beyond their reach. A week ago, he wouldn't have bet a nickel on his chances of being reunited with this mount he had raised from a foal.

"Blizzard out-foxed me, I'll admit," Larbuck said, beating his chest with mittened hands. "When I got to the corral it was beginnin' to snow, but I figgered she would be just a skift. Now I ain't so sure but what you'll be eatin' my beans and bacon for a solid week before you can git to town to see your girl, kid."

An hour later—an incredibly long time to retrace the scant half mile Temple had covered from the ranch house—both men knew the storm had yet to reach its peak, that Temple would be a snowbound guest on S Bar L for several days to come.

They stabled the stallion in Larbuck's lean-to behind the house, in case drifts made it difficult to reach the barn, and retired to the pent-up warmth of the house. As the day ended and the following morning dawned with the snow still falling, Larbuck was quick to observe the impatience which his guest was trying to conceal.

"You're fiddle-footed as a cat on a hot griddle," the old cattleman grunted. "Which is it, boy? Hankerin' to see Avis Malloy, or settle yore business with Karl Gothe over the end of a hot gun?"

Temple glanced up from his job of kneading dubbin into his dried-out cowboots.

"Gothe can wait," the cowpuncher responded. "I suppose I ought to be rarin' to see Avis, Si, but it's clumsy as hell. I mean, knowing Broken Bit belongs to her father, and old Genesee hating my guts like he does."

Larbuck dragged a cotton patch through the smooth bore of his Sharps buffalo rifle, holding it up to squint down the mirror-bright barrel.

"Son, when a man discusses a woman with another man, he's on thin ice. I ain't denyin' Avis ain't the ketch of the pack in these parts. Ain't a two-laiged critter in these foothills who's under eighty that wouldn't want to throw a halter on that schoolmarm like you done."

Larbuck's bright little eyes told Temple that Larbuck was leading up to something he found it hard to approach.

"What are you driving at, Si?"

Larbuck made an unnecessarily elaborate business out of shaving tobacco from a hard black twist to stoke his corncob.

"Avis Malloy visit you while you were in Walla Walla waitin' for execution day, son?"

Temple colored. "No."

"She write often, tellin' you she loved you?" Getting Temple's headshake of negation, Larbuck pressed on: "Why?"

"Jingo Paloo said Genesee wouldn't let her correspond with a condemned convict."

The old S Bar L man sneered noisily. "Tommyrot! Woman loves a man, she'll foller him to hell and back."

After a long run of silence, the old man said carefully, "This Jord Ramont is spendin' the winter at the Trail House, as you know. Room Eight, end of the hall on the second floor, to be exact. Genesee owns the Trail House, so he picked out a room on the ground floor for his quarters. He goes to bed with the chickens, old Genesee does."

Temple said sharply, "Go on with it, Si."

Larbuck snapped his pocketknife shut with a click.

"Avis bunks in Room Six, next door to Ramont. She's young and lonesome and tol'able restless, Buck. Jord Ramont is a handsome young feller, no matter what we think about him and the ruin he aims to bring to this range. Now, who's to say—"

Buck Temple came to his feet, fisting the old man's shirt and lifting Larbuck half off the floor before he controlled his wild surge of temper.

"Si, if you were twenty years younger I'd scrub the floor with your carcass. Mebbe I got cabin fever already. But until I leave this roof, don't let me hear you mention Avis again—or Ramont either. Savvy?"

Larbuck said, "Sure, kid." But for both of them the close rapport of their old friendship was destroyed, perhaps for all time to come.

The snowfall tapered off on the third day, but Temple returned from a scout down the Pass to report that reaching Rimrock, only seven miles distant, would be impossible for a man on horseback.

The following three days, waiting for seasonally warm winds to reopen Coppertooth, Buck Temple occupied himself chopping kindling from

Larbuck's woodpile, stopping that chore only when the supply of wood gave out.

Temple had been an enforced visitor on Larbuck's place for an even week when the Chinook came, and both men knew if the sun held out he would be able to saddle and ride for town by the morrow.

At three o'clock, a barking of dogs and the shrill Texas yipping of Jingo Paloo announced the arrival of the mail courier on his weekly circuit of the foothill's ranches. The empty sled hitched to the dozen huskies which Paloo used to haul the mails in wintertime indicated that Paloo was on the drag end of his circuit.

When the dogs were unhitched and fed their rations in the shelter of Larbuck's barn, Paloo joined Temple and the old rancher at the main house.

"Just come over from Mary Wunderling's homestead," the rangy little mail rider said, his eyes dancing with a sly humor which told Buck Temple that his friend was a bearer of momentous tidings of some sort. "As usual, Mary'd been swappin' heliograph messages with old Cap'n Collie up the Pass, soon as the weather cleared. Buck, I'm happy to say that your manhunt has been taken care of. Yore crusade home has died a-bornin'."

Without asking Paloo, Temple knew that the orphaned girl who lived alone on the homestead under Coppertooth Peak had relayed to Paloo some news bearing on trader Gothe.

"You don't have to talk riddles in front of Si," Temple said impatiently.

Paloo backed up to the fireplace and rested his puckish gaze on the cedar-stocked Peacemaker belted to Temple's thigh.

"You can rub Karl Gothe's monicker off o' that bullet we were discussin' on Winn's stage the other day, Buck. Karl Gothe is now a name on a boothill headboard. As of a week ago last night."

Si Larbuck saw the strained fixture come to Temple's mouth as he digested this news, reading the stunned disappointment of a man who had come back to this country with vengeance as his prime motive.

"Gothe's dead?" Larbuck asked.

Paloo ducked his head. "As a sheep tick in creosote, mister. Shot betwixt the eyes, on the steps in front of the Mile-High. They buried him yesterday."

Buck Temple dragged a hand across his jaw, eyes drilling into the mail rider's beaming face.

"Anybody know who done it?" Larbuck wanted to know.

Paloo grinned mysteriously, like a washerwoman with a juicy morsel of neighborhood gossip on the tip of her tongue.

"Indeed, yes, my friends. Cap'n Collie witnessed the shootin'. Fact is, Collie's the main

61

witness at the killer's trial, which is goin' on at this time in the county courthouse."

Si Larbuck made a despairing gesture. "All right, you damned Indian. Feed it to us by drops. Who shot Gothe?"

The mirth left Paloo's face now. His eyes were fixed on Buck Temple with a wedging gravity.

"You can't guess?"

Temple spoke for the first time. "I haven't the foggiest notion who they'd arrest for shooting that trader."

"Well, it was Jord Ramont."

An abrupt change came to Buck Temple now. He said hoarsely, "You mean they're trying Ramont for Gothe's murder on the testimony of an old soak like Collie?"

"That's how she stacks up, Mary said."

"No jury would convict a man on the evidence of that man," Larbuck grunted. "Collie could have said a three pronged octopusk wrung Gothe's fat neck with as much foundation in truth."

Paloo stared down at the growing puddles around his boots.

"Well, anyhow, accordin' to what Cap'n Collie signaled down to Mary this mornin', the case goes to the jury today. The bettin' element don't give Ramont a chance to beat the noose."

Buck Temple shook himself out of his deep study with a visible effort.

"Ramont had no motive for killing Gothe. Not after Gothe sold Broken Bit to a man who's turning over my timber rights to Ramont. Collie was either lying or too drunk to identify the killer."

Jingo Paloo shrugged. "Anyhow, Ramont couldn't establish an alibi for where he was at the time of the shootin'. That was around midnight on Wednesday, just as the blizzard broke."

Buck Temple crossed over to the corner where his high-horned Pendleton stock saddle had been pegged since last fall.

"I'm heading for town," he told Larbuck. "Thanks for putting me up. And don't forget our Cattlemen's meeting here at your place soon as the weather clears. Regardless of what happens to Ramont, his timber company can still ruin us."

Temple slammed the big slab door behind him, heading for the lean-to and his blue stallion.

"First break of good luck that boy has had since Gothe claimed he seen Buck shoot that timber cruiser," Si Larbuck said jubilantly. "You know what it means if Jord Ramont hangs, Jingo? It means his loggin' outfit will fold up and us ranchers will be spared a bloody war this summer. Which we prob'ly would have lost, even with Buck to ramrod us."

Jingo Paloo stepped to a window and watched Buck Temple ride past the house on his way toward the Pass road.

"It also means that Buck won't have any competition where Avis Malloy is concerned," the mail courier drawled with a troubled inflection coloring his words. "Not that that woman is good enough to polish Buck's boots."

A disturbing thought came to Larbuck in this moment.

"I hope the sheriff keeps an eye on Buck when he shows up in town tonight," the S Bar L rancher said. "I got a hunch Jord Ramont has left standin' orders for his loggers to bushwhack that kid first chance they git."

Chapter 5

Riding into town, Buck Temple found Rimrock sprawled brooding and spectral beneath the high-wheeling March moon, its unpainted shacks showing no lights under the frowning backdrop of the Pass cliffs. Only the courthouse was alive tonight; its upper tier of windows were yellow rectangles framing the silhouettes of standees rimming the courtroom walls.

He found a space for his blue roan at the stake-and-rider fence surrounding the courthouse square, and threaded his way through the double ranks of hacks and buckboards parked hub to hub along the street.

Obviously, the news of Jord Ramont's murder trial had traveled up and down the foothill country, like the spread of a ripple across a quiet pool. There could be no other explanation for such a concentration of saddle horses and wagons in town, so soon after the blizzard's release.

Cattle had been the genesis of this isolated town, and every cattle brand along the foothills was represented here tonight. These men, recognizing in Jord Ramont the worst threat the security of their range had yet known, had assembled here to witness the outcome of their enemy's trial.

Mounting the courthouse steps, Temple had his nostalgic view of the town's wide street, so vividly drawn in his memory during the winter months behind bars.

The massive shape of Genesee Malloy's Trail House Hotel cut its hard square angles at the corner of Main and B, the largest building in town. The windows of the principal saloons—the Timberline, the Index, the Cowboys' Club—were dark for the first time in Temple's recollection.

Snowdrifts remained unshoveled under the wooden awning of Karl Gothe's store, their gray gleam relieving the monotonous hues of a street churned to quagmire by hoofed and wheeled traffic since the snows had melted before this week's Chinook.

Temple turned to the vestibule doors and found them unlocked and unattended. Lamps glittered in wall sconces along the hall, doors opening on the offices of the recorder and assessor, the tax collector, and other county officials.

He took a flight of spur-scuffed steps up the clock tower to the top landing facing the courtroom doors. As he reached this landing a sudden burst of sound came from the packed courtroom, sound unleashed by a gavel's dismissive rapping. Court had been adjourned or recessed.

The big double doors of the hall of justice slammed open to disgorge a motley crowd—

timber ranchers belonging to the Foothill Association, lumbermen looking strangely foreign in their high-laced boots and red shirts, hired by the hated Ramont Timber Company; housewives in shawls and gingham, red-faced townsmen in their black coats and beaver hats.

Except for the loggers, Buck Temple knew most of these people, knew their individual backgrounds intimately. The generation he had gone to school with, approaching their thirties now, formed one segment of this perspiring courtroom audience; the balding heads and shaggy beards of the oldsters brought memories of his own boyhood to Temple now.

He knew he had become a marked man in this community, and having no desire to weather the storm of congratulations which he knew these cow country people would heap upon him, Temple moved back into a shadow-clotted corner to escape discovery, away from the tide of humanity spilling down the narrow stairs.

Scraps of talk, eager and violent, hushed and somber, touched his ears in a steady din as the crowd passed.

"I say Ramont's neck is as good as stretched. Why you suppose he kept mum about where he was at the time?"

"Hell, Amos, the sheriff testified that Jordan wasn't in his hotel room ten minutes after old Collie seen him shoot Gothe. That proves—"

A woman's voice, shrill and vindictive, "My dear, did you notice how pale the Malloy girl looked? Like a sheet, I do declare. Do you suppose—"

Temple's eyes, shadowed under the downsweep of his Stetson, searched the passing throng, seeking the girl's face that had haunted him, asleep and awake, since the moment of their parting four months ago under the roof of this very courthouse.

When the last man had stumbled down the steps to leave the courtroom gallery empty, Temple knew he had missed Avis Malloy. There were side exits to this building; no doubt his fiancée and her crusty old sire had chosen one of them to avoid the congestion at the main exit.

Oppressed by a vague sense of disappointment, Temple stepped into the courtroom, his face sagging and wholly without expression as his gaze shuttled along the area beyond the railing where the attorneys in the case were scooping papers off their tables.

Mose Hartley, sheriff's deputy, was stationed at the door marked JURY ROOM, evidence that the jury hearing Ramont's case had retired behind locked doors to ponder the lumberman's fate. Temple saw the black-robed figure of the circuit judge disappear through the door of his private chambers. There was no sign of Sheriff John "Canuck" Brockway or his prisoner; by now the

68

lawman had removed Jord Ramont to the jail wing downstairs.

When the attorneys had left the echoing room, Temple headed down the central aisle, the impounded animal heat of the day-long trial impinging itself with a fetid thickness on his nostrils.

Immediately behind the judge's bench and below the huge American flag which dominated the back wall was the doorway which Temple knew led to the backstairs and the jail; he had traveled that same route, manacled to Brockway's wrist, five months before.

Mose Hartley spotted him from his post beside the jury room door and cried out his surprise. "Buck Temple, by God! When'd you git back, boy?"

Temple said, "See you later, Mose," and ducked through the door behind the bench into the lamp-lit chill of the back staircase.

In the annex below, Buck Temple entered the sheriff's office and found it deserted. He was staring about at the well-remembered details of this room, the gun cabinet and the reward posters tacked to the faded wallpaper, when the bull-pen door opened and the tall shape of Canuck Brockway entered, a lantern bail looped over his arm, his star flashing from a gallus strap.

"Well, Buck, God bless you! I've prayed for this handshake many's the time this winter."

"Canuck, old hoss, how are you?"

They had always been as close as father and son, these two. Brockway was a salty old Canadian, not looking his seventy odd years. Sprays of crowfoot wrinkles fanned from the corners of his deep-socketed eyes; an inverted crescent of mustache ambushed a mouth where a smile could generally be found lurking. A former redcoat with the Northwest Mounted Police, he had drifted south of the British Columbia border to become a Yankee by adoption, a bred-in-the-bone law officer who had worn Rimrock's star for a generation.

It was Canuck Brockway who had helped young Buck, then a husky stripling of fifteen, pack old Gideon Temple out of the hills, when Buck's father had been crushed in a rockslide while chousing steers out of a gully during a calf round-up. It was this same sheriff who had been Buck's escort across the desert last fall on that fateful journey to the Territorial penitentiary.

"What's the lowdown on Ramont, Sheriff?"

Brockway blinked the mist out of his eyes.

"The judge has recessed the court until the jury brings in a verdict. The crowd's gone out to grab a bite of supper. They'll be back in an hour. I got my doubts about the jury bein' deadlocked after the first ballot."

Temple's hand dropped to his side as the old sheriff finally let go his grip.

70

"The case is that conclusive, is it?"

Brockway nodded, his eyes touching Temple here and there, hungrily as a father might inspect a long-absent son.

"Well, Ramont had no defense to offer. Claimed he was out taking a walk at the time of Gothe's murder. I picked him up in his room at the Trail House a couple hours after the shooting. Apparently he hadn't arranged an alibi with his logging crew, who were playing poker at the Timberline. I had my deputy covering the place, just in case."

Temple was tight-lipped and silently contemplative as he watched the grizzled old lawman lock up his keys in the safe.

"But what did the prosecutor establish as Ramont's motive for wanting Gothe out of the way, Sheriff? It doesn't tie together. That pair were thick as thieves from the moment Ramont first showed up in Rimrock."

The rawboned old Canadian fished a turnip watch from his pocket and consulted the time.

"I think you lie at the bottom of that, Buck," the sheriff said cryptically. "Seen Avis yet?"

"No. I just rode in."

"Got time to run over to Straight-Edge Josie's house? Or will you be wanting to look up Avis at the hotel?"

Sensing the answer old Brockway wanted, Temple put aside the restive urgency that was in him to feel Avis Malloy in his arms again. He said, "I'd like to see that message Bluedom left before he committed suicide, if it's still there. I would be six feet under if it hadn't been for that."

The sheriff took his fleece coat off a wall rack and shucked into it.

"Bluedom's scribble is still there. The coroner's jury went over to inspect it under guard." Brockway chuckled as he and Temple left the jail by a side door. "First time old Tex Waterby and Grandpa Hutchins had ever been inside a bawdy house to hear them tell it."

Sloshing through the mud of the courthouse yard, heading toward the upper edge of town where Straight-Edge Josie had her notorious establishment, Temple asked, "Any loggers on the jury, Sheriff?"

Again that short laugh. "Nary a one. Couldn't qualify, not bein' bona fide residents of the county. You know, it's as if Ramont's perfectly sure he'll be acquitted, weak as his defense was. From the first, he's been cool as a cucumber."

They had now reached Straight-Edge Josie's bagnio at the foot of the talus hill. The sheriff walked in without knocking, ignoring the jabbering girls assembled around Madame Josie's parlor fireplace, their cheeks flushed from their recent walk over from the courthouse.

At the far end of a murky upstairs hall, the sheriff took a padlock key from his pocket and opened the door of a crib which emitted the stale smells compounded of whisky and perfume and unaired bedclothing.

Brockway lighted a lamp on a shabby marble-top washstand, and its feeble glare accentuated the bleakness of these tawdry surroundings where a conscience-stricken murderer had blown out his brains less than a month ago.

The mattress ticking on the brass bedstead was still smudged with brown bloodstains where Vance Bluedom's body had been found. On the oatmeal wallpaper beside the bed, Temple read the almost illegible scrawl which the timber faller had scribbled there with the point of a soft-nose cartridge.

2—23—87. I was paid $500 dolars to bushwhack Les McAlster.

Vance Bluedom.

Those were the words which had removed a hang rope from Buck Temple's neck. The spell of them subdued his spirit as Brockway blew out the lamp and joined him in the hall, both men glad to be out of that room, away from its shady secrets of men's lusts and its evidence of violent death.

"Too bad Bluedom didn't tell *who* paid him to kill McAllister," Brockway said, when they were once more outside the brothel.

"I'm lucky he was sober enough to write what he did, Sheriff."

They turned their steps toward Main Street, now aglow with blooming lamplight along its entire length.

"Who'd have that kind of money to railroad you, Buck? Who'd gain the most by having you out of the way? Jord Ramont."

Temple shook himself out of gloomy introspection.

"Bluedom was a faller drawing Ramont's pay," the sheriff went on. "You were the one cattleman with the guts to fight this timber-steal business. Ramont wanted the timber in Glacier Canyon, on your Broken Bit range. Is this thing so hard to figger out?"

Temple said heavily, "Les McAllister was drawing Ramont's pay, too. It was McAllister's cruise that located the timber on my spread. Where does Karl Gothe fit into all this?"

Brockway grunted, feeling the exertion of their uphill trek.

"Why, McAllister had served his purpose. Ramont knew he was the most logical man to bait your trap. McAllister was bushwhacked on your range, Ramont had a prominent citizen handy to pin the killing on you. It worked out, didn't it? Ramont owns the timber rights to Broken Bit now. Gothe arranged that."

At the edge of Main Street, alongside the Mile-

High Mercantile, Temple drew up, turning to face his old friend.

"But what bearing does all this puzzle-solving have on the fact that Karl Gothe was killed?"

The sheriff took a cigar out of his pocket, bit off the end, and stuck it in his teeth.

"Well, folks around here think Ramont paid Gothe to sell you down the river last fall, Buck. Folks think Gothe was wise to Ramont's hand being back of Bluedom being the real killer, from the first. With you due to show up again after that suicide changed everything, Ramont had to get Gothe out of the way before you forced the truth out of him. We'll see how the jury adds it up, Buck."

Temple sucked in a slow breath, his gaze straying over to the lighted lobby of the Trail House, up to the shuttered window of Avis Malloy's room on the top floor. He was recalling Si Larbuck's slanderous innuendo in this moment, and the memory of it put a darkening flush over his features, knowing the town shared Larbuck's opinions of Avis's fidelity. Jord Ramont's window was right beside Avis's.

"Get along and see your girl," Canuck Brockway's gentle voice broke into his stream of thought. "You'll bed down with us tonight. I'll have Aunt Molly fix up the spare room."

Leaving Brockway, Temple crossed the empty street with long strides, feeling the sense of a man nearing the end of a long and grueling journey. Entering the Trail House lobby, he found it crowded with men and women discussing the Ramont trial, the air electric with the criss-crossing excitements of a Roman holiday which ruled this cow town tonight.

The gaunt-cheeked, white-headed figure of Genesee Malloy intercepted Temple as he headed for the stairway immediately beyond Malloy's reception desk. This man—a veteran lumberman before he had come to Rimrock to buy the hotel and retire on its income—had the face of Lincoln, and the surly temper of a man who had found life too sour for his liking.

All of Malloy's malice was in his eyes now as he blocked Temple at the foot of the stairs.

"Where do you think you're going, Buck?"

"Avis is in her room. I'm going up."

Malloy's jaw hardened. "Like hell. I'll have no convict calling publicly for my daughter this way."

Temple's hands fisted at his sides. He was aware of heads turning to stare at him; several called his name in excited tones as they saw the key figure in the town's drama standing here in their midst.

"Genesee, step aside. If you were younger, I'd knock you aside."

His shoulder met Malloy's with a solid blow; the old man was swiveled around, and he made no move to halt the tall cowpuncher as Temple headed up the stairs three steps at a time.

At the door of Room Six, Temple stood a moment staring at Avis Malloy's card tacked to the panels. During their courtship days, when Avis had been the town schoolteacher, Buck had never deigned to invade the privacy of the girl's boudoir in this fashion; he had always waited for her downstairs, knowing the cruel venom which cow town gossip could inflict on a woman's good name.

Now he found himself rapping at her door, aware of the leaping surge of long pent-up hungers which he had forced into the background of his mind during the long weeks at Walla Walla.

The door opened and Avis stood there, unprepared for this meeting. Surprise put its mark on her full ripe lips; in the shocked incredulity of her wide and gentian-blue eyes.

The rear lighting of her ceiling lamp put a halo around the fringes of her upswept, raven-black hair; she had thrown a dressing robe of plum-colored velvet over her street clothes, the garment belted loosely over the full curves of her body.

"Buck! Oh, my darling, Buck!"

They were in each other's arms then, there in the doorway, oblivious of all else in the world as their lips met in the heated pressure of their love for each other, as their arms drew them hungrily together.

The heady scent of her hair was a poignant, remembered sweetness in his nostrils, enflaming his blood; the taut pressure of her high-modeled breasts sent maddening desire through every fiber of his being.

When finally he released her, Avis pulled him into the room and shut the door on the babble from the lobby downstairs. Long afterward, it seemed, they found time for words to replace the testimony their eyes and hearts had exchanged in this new-found togetherness, doubly sweet after all that had gone before.

He noted now that Avis Malloy's eyes were swollen and red-rimmed from recent weeping; and the edge went out of this reunion for him, guessing at the cause of her grief.

Seated on a sofa backed against the street windows, Temple saw that she no longer wore the ring he had squandered half his last year's beef receipts to buy for her in Tacoma, as the pledge of his betrothal. He saw Avis drop her glance, reading his thought.

"Dad refused to let me wear it after you left," she whispered tensely. "The same way he wouldn't let me write you in Walla Walla this winter, Buck. You've got to believe that."

Knots of muscle swelled and hardened at the corner of his jaw. Basically, he understood

Genesee Malloy's motives; the man had opposed his daughter's courtship to this small-tally cowman from the outset, having higher ambitions for her. But there was something Temple had to know; and because he was a man of simple and direct impulses, he made no effort to approach that question by roundabout tangents now.

"Does Jord Ramont's future mean so much to you, Avis?"

She looked up quickly, her eyes haunted and somehow unsure of how to answer his blunt query.

"Buck, don't misunderstand what I am going to tell you. But Jord is being crucified by this town's hatred for any man who isn't a cattle rancher." She broke off, seizing his hands in hers. "Buck, *Jord didn't shoot Karl Gothe.* I don't know who did, but Captain Collie lied. Jord is innocent."

Buck Temple searched the eyes of this girl he loved for a full minute before he spoke. "You're so sure? Why?"

"Buck, if Karl Gothe was shot at midnight, or an hour before then, or an hour after, Jord had no part in it."

"How do you know that, Avis?"

Her bosom heaved to a deep intake of breath. "Because—*because Jord Ramont was visiting me in this very room during those two hours of that night,* Buck. Please, in God's name, don't think the wrong thing of me."

Temple stood up, breaking her grasp on his big wrists.

"You could have been Jord Ramont's alibi in court, then. Why didn't you defend him, Avis? Isn't a man's life—any man's life—worth the disgrace that would have brought you?"

Avis Malloy came to her feet, her cheeks marble white and glistening now with fresh tears.

"Jord made me promise, Buck. He held his own tongue in defense of my honor. He—we both heard the sheriff go to his room, after the shooting. We didn't know then what for."

Temple swept his Stetson off a table and turned to the door, his brain too confused to think this thing out now. Her voice followed him, pleading and tragic.

"Buck, if you love me—as I love you—don't let this terrible thing come between us. Promise me you'll see that the sheriff never reaches Walla Walla with Jord as his prisoner, if the jury finds him guilty tonight!"

Looking into Avis Malloy's eyes, reading the torture which lay naked on her soul for him to see, Buck Temple pulled the girl into his arms, rubbed his stubby cheek against the satin texture of her own.

"I wouldn't be half a man if I didn't have faith in the girl I aim to marry," he said finally. "Ramont won't hang for this thing, Avis. I'll get him away from Brockway."

He left her then, afraid to trust his own desires; he left the Trail House by way of an outdoor fire escape to avoid a second meeting with Genesee Malloy.

He was pacing the floor of Ma Brockway's spare bedroom when, shortly before midnight, he heard the sheriff come home from the courthouse. Stepping to the door, Buck Temple heard the old lawman make his succinct report to his wife.

"Jury found Ramont guilty as charged, Molly. Unanimous on the third ballot. I'll be taking him to Walla Walla day after tomorrow to hang."

Chapter 6

Avis Malloy appeared at the sheriff's home next morning just as white-haired Aunt Molly, Brockway's motherly wife, was serving breakfast to Canuck and Buck Temple.

"You're taking Mr. Ramont outside in a day or two," the girl said when the amenities were over. "You wouldn't mind if I saw him in his cell before you leave, would you?"

Canuck Brockway did not look up from his plate.

"Would your father approve you visiting a condemned murderer in my jail, Avis?"

The girl shrugged. "It's only because Dad has to know where to ship his belongings from the hotel, Canuck."

Buck Temple avoided the girl's gaze. He thought, Avis wants to let Ramont know I've promised to get him away from the sheriff on the way out.

Later, escorting Avis back to the Trail House, Temple got her frank confirmation as to her reason for wanting to visit Ramont in his jail cell.

"In return for saving his life, Buck, I'm positive Jord will withdraw his timber company from the foothills," she told him eagerly. "That's the bargain I'll put to him. You see what you stand to gain, Buck? No trees cut, no cattle war. No bloodshed, no grieving widows—perhaps myself included. Oh, Buck, you won't regret doing this thing."

Halting outside the hotel entrance, Temple shook tobacco into a trough of paper between his fingers, and said drily, "Ramont has no choice but to get out of the Territory, Avis. Once freed, he'll have to go on the dodge. Saving him from Brockway won't alter the jury's verdict or the judge's sentence."

He cemented the cigarette with his tongue and turned as if to leave her. She caught his arm.

"Buck, we have so much to talk about. The things you'll want me to tell Jord. Our own future plans. Everything—"

Temple's scowl was hidden behind a spout of tobacco smoke.

"You can tell Ramont," he said, "that I'll stop the stage at the foot of the Pass, where the coach will be at a crawl rounding the Grapevine Curve. Tell him I'll have a horse ready for his getaway. The rest is up to him."

She saw him go down the steps, his broad back rebuking her, showing his disillusion and his doubts more clearly than words could have done. Her eyes followed the big man across the ankle deep mud of Main Street, until he was lost to view in the center of a crowd of ranchmen who, spotting him from the windows of the Timberline Saloon, had trooped out to welcome him back to his home range.

It gave Avis Malloy pause, this striking proof of the weight her fiancé pulled in this country, his personality towering over his kind like a tall pine in second-growth brush. These rough and bearded foothill cattlemen were welcoming Temple home like a hero back from the wars. Young he might be, a rancher without a ranch; but Buck Temple was the only man to rally them, the only leader, in an hour when leadership was vital to their destiny.

Genesee Malloy joined her on the hotel porch, guessed her mood and commented softly, "Buck ain't worth your tears, Avie. You weren't meant to be a two-bit ranchman's squaw, slavin' the rest of your life to keep body and soul together. Temple's shown he can't pan out the kind of color you deserve in a husband."

Turning to face Genesee's spare, austere mien, his daughter said, half to herself, "If I could be sure, Dad. If I could only be sure you're right about Buck before I cut away from him."

In the privacy of a gambling cubicle off the Timberline barroom, facing the men he had planned to meet at Si Larbuck's ranch for a council of war, Temple spoke the doubts which ruled him.

"Ramont's finished, and most of you are thinking our fight for survival has been avoided," he said gravely. "When you get back to your homes, I want each of you to warn your crews that our range is not yet safe. Ramont Timber Company has a fat contract with Pacific & Western. His loggers can carry on after Ramont is gone."

Grizzled old Texas Sam Waterby, at eighty the oldest cowman in this group, voiced a matter which was in every heart. "Your Broken Bit spread is the weak link in this set-up, Buck, as long as Genesee Malloy holds title to that timber in Glacier Canyon. You got to get Broken Bit back. It's the only way to keep lumberin' interests from gettin' a toe hold in the heart of our graze. Can you do it?"

Temple's eyes were clouded over.

"It's no secret that Genesee doesn't cotton to taking me on as a son-in-law. He has bigger dreams for her. Now that I own nothing but my horse and saddle and the clothes on my back, do you think Malloy would give up his hold over me?"

Buck Temple shoved back his chair, restlessness crowding him hard even in this circle of tried and trusted friends.

"The real timber belt is the foothill strip between our west boundaries and the High Rim," he said. "Si Larbuck has hinted that some of you ranch owners are willing to lease your timber rights to Ramont. Is Larbuck wrong?"

The assembled ranchers stirred uneasily. One of them, Hal Dikus, whose Lazy D outfit adjoined Broken Bit on the south, said defiantly:

"What's to keep Ramont's company, or any other loggin' outfit, from cuttin' the government forest above our spreads? All he'd have to do is move his loggers out o' Glacier Canyon onto timber that we don't control."

Tex Waterby cut in angrily, "That's the key to the whole problem, Dikus. Suppose that government timber is logged off? We depend on that timber to keep our foothill graze from bein' washed plumb to the ocean by the spring thaws."

Hal Dikus got to his feet, shame showing on his cheeks, defiance in his eyes.

"I say that Ramont's bunch will ruin us anyhow," the Lazy D man said. "He's offered me ten thousand in cash for what timber I own, because it's easier to log off than the timber he could lease from the government. I don't see why I shouldn't grab that money. Lazy D won't be worth hell-room when the trees are stripped off o' the hills above me nohow."

Sizing up this crowd of representative ranchmen, Buck Temple saw that Si Larbuck's appraisal of their loyalties and shifting allegiances had been all too accurate.

"We're too few here to decide this thing today,"

Temple snapped. "Si Larbuck is president of our Association. He'll be sending word to you about a mass meeting at S Bar L for early next week. We'll decide where we stand on this range war then."

Wheeling as he reached the door of the gambling room, Temple addressed the cattlemen with harsh emphasis. "Regardless of how many of us sell out to the lumbermen who aim to ruin our range, I'm going to fight until the last logger has dragged his ax out of these hills. And I don't even own a ranch."

Temple's abrupt departure left a brooding vacuum in the room, an embarrassed silence which was finally broken by Joe Redwine, boss of the Rocking R outfit on Arrowhead Creek.

"You'd almost think Buck was sorry we put a noose around Ramont's craw," mused the cowman, who had been jury foreman.

Tex Waterby snorted. "You so thick you don't know the burr under his saddle, Joe? Ramont's conviction leaves the issue between the Malloy girl and Buck hangin' fire. If Buck don't know Ramont was makin' a play for his woman, he soon will. With Ramont in boothill, how's Buck to know which was her first choice? That worm will gnaw him to his dyin' day, no matter how good a wife she makes him."

That night at supper, Buck Temple announced to Aunt Molly and the sheriff that he was pulling out at dawn tomorrow to ride circuit on the foothill outfits, spreading the word of the forthcoming Cattlemen's Association meeting at Larbuck's.

In reality, he was making his plans to be away from Rimrock when the sheriff left town in Billy Winn's stage, with Jord Ramont as his prisoner. It put a pang of guilt in Temple's heart, thus deceiving his kindly old host; but barring unforeseen accident, the old lawman would never know who wielded the gun which would free Ramont from his custody tomorrow.

Temple went to bed early, borrowing Aunt Molly's alarm clock and setting it for an hour before daylight. It was fifty miles to the last ranch in the foothill string, Waterby's Diamond X; for that reason alone, neither the sheriff nor his wife would see anything unusual about his wanting to make an early start.

Temple had his bad moment when, roused by the alarm and after dressing in total darkness, he found Aunt Molly preparing breakfast for him out in the kitchen.

The gray light of the false dawn was already showing beyond the notch of Coppertooth Pass when Temple saddled Blue in the sheriff's private stable and turned the big stallion to Main Street.

Rimrock showed no sign of life as Temple paid his surreptitious visit to the Trail House stable, throwing a saddle on Jord Ramont's big

Appaloosa gelding. During the night, Avis had lashed the lumberman's bedroll and saddlebags to the hull; and she was waiting in the semi-darkness when Temple led the two horses out through the rear of the hotel barn.

"I can't waste time now, Avis," Temple greeted her with a certain roughness entering his voice as she clung to him, kissing him passionately. "This whole deal will go sour if anyone in town sees me making off with Ramont's saddler."

She withdrew from him, offended by his curt-ness, her breath steaming in the brisk morning cold.

"You understand why this has to be, Buck? You will have no regrets?"

He swung into stirrups, dallying the Appa-loosa's lead rope around his saddle horn.

"No regrets, Avis. You say Ramont is innocent, and I believe you."

He spurred off up the ridge to put Rimrock out of sight behind a flank of the Pass cliffs; and was a good mile away from the cow town before dawn reached the Cascades in its full glittering light.

By the time that sun was an hour high he had dropped a thousand feet, paralleling the Pass road; at noon he crossed that road at a point above Si Larbuck's ranch, scouting the open Pass with extreme care before crossing it.

He felt some slight concern over the trail he

had left behind him, in case Sheriff Brockway decided to start his manhunt from the Trail House barn. It was Temple's design to head north as soon as his business with Ramont had been accomplished at the Grapevine Curve. He wanted to spend the night at Tex Waterby's place, fifty miles north; that would be in his favor when Sheriff Brockway started trying to think this thing out.

But there was little chance that Brockway would ever link Temple with the stage holdup this afternoon; the whole thing was too preposterous to enter his old friend's head. Buck Temple stood to gain the most from Ramont's departure, both from the cattle war angle and for personal reasons.

By one o'clock, Buck Temple had followed the canyon of Arrowhead Creek to the base of Coppertooth Peak's thousand foot lava spire. Ahead was the old Wunderling homestead, where a retired military surgeon from Custer's regiment had brought his wife and daughter to the Cascade foothills, shortly after the massacre on the Little Bighorn.

Temple made a dry camp in the timber which shut off his view from the Wunderling home-stead, the self-same pines where Yakima Indian renegades had gathered for their attack, five years ago, on the Wunderlings. Old Major Wunderling and his wife had lost their scalps in that raid; their daughter Mary, then a girl in her early teens, had miraculously escaped, the details of her ordeal not clearly known to her neighbors.

Taking no chances on the Ellensburg stage having pulled out of Rimrock ahead of schedule, Temple arrived at the Grapevine Curve at the foot of the Pass at two-thirty; the stage was due here at three.

He picketed Ramont's gelding and his own blue roan in a clump of bushes fifty yards off the road. Knowing his new Stetson was something the sheriff would be sure to recognize, Temple wrapped a bandanna around his head and used another bandanna to mask his face.

His long-skirted oilskin saddle slicker formed the remainder of his disguise; it was a universal garment in this country and would give Brockway no distinguishing features to remember later.

Shortly before three o'clock, Temple heard the echoing clatter of Billy Winn's stage rushing down the Pass grade. Crouched behind a deadfull spruce at the turn of the Grapevine, a Winchester carbine at his side, Temple waited as the mud-spattered Concord came in sight upgrade, old Winn riding the brake and holding his span of Morgans in tight check.

Nearing the Grapevine's tight hairpin curve, Winn brought the team to a momentary dead halt, reset his brake, and then gathered his lines to resume the tight turn. It was at this precisely awaited moment that Buck Temple vaulted over the snow-crusted stump of the deadfall and laid his gun sights on Sheriff Canuck Brockway, peering through the open window of the coach.

Billy Winn, an old hand at holdups, promptly wrapped his ribbons around his Jacob's staff and raised his arms.

"You drawed a blank this run, my friend," the old reinsman drawled. "I'm carryin' no express box."

Altering his voice to a throaty caw, Temple put his order to the sheriff. "Step out with your hands in sight."

After a moment's delay, the stage door swung open and Jord Ramont, bundled in a plucked beaver coat, jumped to the ground. His right wrist was fettered to Brockway's left. A high flush was on the lumberman's cheeks; he stared at the masked man on the stump with jaw sagging in well-feigned surprise.

Sheriff Brockway's rheumy eyes searched the slicker-clad road agent with a careful wariness as he dismounted from the stage, leaving his sawed-off shotgun inside.

"Unlock the bracelets," Temple ordered in the same grating, half-muffled voice.

Anger purpled the old Canadian's cheeks as he realized this was no routine holdup. The stage had been halted to remove a prisoner bound to Walla Walla and the gallows. Up on the box, Billy Winn stopped masticating his cud of tobacco, surprise showing on his saturnine features.

Brockway produced a key and unsnapped the notched jaws of Ramont's half of the handcuffs. At once the lumberman flung himself across the road, scrambling over the rotten deadfall to catch Temple's whispered order: "Your bronc's in the bushes yonder. I'll hold the sheriff ten minutes."

Behind him, Temple heard Ramont clawing his way through the heavy brush to the waiting horses.

"Turn around," Temple ordered the sheriff, "and belly up to the wheel. Don't budge for ten minutes. I'll have the two of you covered that long. Driver, don't start your team till you get my signal from the ridge."

Sheriff Brockway turned to face the Concord; at that instant, the quiet of this mountain gap was rudely breached by the sudden crash of a rifle, from the edge of the timber somewhere above the road.

Ramont had not fired that shot; Temple had left no weapon in the saddle boot of either horse. He saw Sheriff Brockway lurch to the impact of a slug in the back, saw his old friend slump face downward between the stage wheels.

In the space of an eyewink, Buck Temple heard the following shot and saw Billy Winn pitched lifeless into the stage boot, his skull drilled from temple to temple by a steel-jacketed bullet.

The stage team, panicked by the clashing echoes of those two gunshots, broke into a runaway gallop from a standing start, the mud-stoppered hind wheels crunching over Brockway's legs as he lay sprawled under the Concord.

Sick with a leaping consternation, Buck Temple wheeled around on the stump to see Jord Ramont spurring his Appaloosa up the slope, riding to meet three bandanna-masked horsemen who had broken free of the snow-draped undergrowth.

Temple opened his mouth to yell, at the same time hearing the scream of Morgans and the crash of wood and metal as the Rimrock stage, failing to negotiate the tight Grapevine bend, careened off the road behind him.

He saw smoke spurt from the muzzle of a rifle up there on the ridge, ahead of Ramont; and simultaneously Temple felt himself knocked off the log by the jarring impact of a bullet drilling his belly.

Instinct drove Temple to pick himself up and, leaving his Winchester behind, slog through the hedge to where Blue stood waiting. Badly hit, Temple was vaguely aware of hearing Ramont's shout of "Get Temple!" blending with those of the trio of ambushers higher up the slope.

Somehow he was in saddle, and Blue was streaking off down a trackless expanse of unmelted snow toward the nearby rim of the forest.

A hundred yards from the road, Buck Temple's senses skidded over the rim of a spinning black funnel. He had no knowledge of pitching from stirrups; the snowbank into which he plummeted completely covered his diving body.

The big blue stallion raced off and away into the dark timber, empty stirrups swinging, snagging brush. It was the sound of Blue's headlong flight over the rocky terrain below that sent Jord Ramont and his trio of rescuers hammering in pursuit, their shortcut to intercept the blue roan leading them well away from the snowbank which concealed the body of their fallen quarry.

Long afterward, the sounds of the chase died off, muffled behind the thick curtains of the roundabout forest. The last malignant echo was rejected by the volcano lift of Coppertooth Peak. And the silence of death rushed in to fill the crisp vacuum of the scene.

Chapter 7

The cedar shakes and peeled-pole rafters above Temple's head were alternately bronze and ebony in the shuttering glare of a nearby fireplace. This rock-walled cabin contained the mingled aroma of wood-smoke and leather, the tantalizing effluvium of whatever was stewing in the hearth pot, and the subtle turpentine-sharp smell of pine cones.

He moved his head experimentally on a pillow fluffy with goosedown. He realized then that he was stretched out on a rawhide-slatted bed, a blue army blanket draped over him.

There was a sticky dry fur in Buck Temple's mouth which told of a fever recently broken. When he groped a hand out from under the blanket it was to find his jaw stubbled with a full half-inch growth of curly, wire-stiff black whiskers. He couldn't account for the time it had taken to produce that beard.

He was not aware of drifting back to sleep; when he awakened again there was a throbbing agony beating somewhere core-deep in his side. And the firelight no longer danced on the rafters up there. Daylight filled the room with its vital brilliance.

A cool breeze, spiced with the smell of snow

and pines, ruffled the flowered calico curtains of an open window above his bed. Through that aperture in the mortared lava rock wall, Buck Temple squinted at a shaft of sunlight pouring steeply into the cabin, dust particles swimming golden in suspension there.

Gradually, focusing his eyes to further distance, he recognized the swaying crowns of tall timber outside; masking out his view of blue sky was a solid vertical barrier of eroded and lichen-seamed rock of a peculiar coffee-color.

"Coppertooth Peak," he thought, knowing that only one landmark had this peculiar coloring; and the knowledge comforted him, giving him his first link with reality, his first definite orientation. It brought back a dim and disordered recollection of the shooting on the Pass road, of feeling Blue's reaching gallop under him. Memory hit dead end with that scene.

Every pulse of his heart was like a hot blade twisting in his guts. The pain of it wrenched a moan from his lips and when he jerked his head spasmodically around on the pillow he got his first glimpse of the girl at the foot of the bed.

She carried a steaming bowl of water in her hands, a towel draped over one arm. Her eyes, regarding him with an alert inquiry, were the shade of a mountain pool in springtime-deep jade, bright and alive. Eyes set in a well-modeled face, with cheeks and forehead stained a vital bronze hue that owed its translucent beauty to no cosmetics.

Her face was framed in a thick shoulder-length bob of high-sheened chestnut hair, caught back from her ears by a bandeau of bright cloth such as an Indian might wear. The thought occurred to him that she might be some uncommonly beautiful squaw, for her high-breasted torso was clad in fringed buckskin, its laced front dipping below the rim of the basin she had just brought over from the hearth.

"You could do with a shave, Buck Temple."

Only by the movement of her full wide mouth was the man aware that she was speaking to him; the rush of blood tom-tomming in his ears was that insistent, that loud.

He ran his tongue over his lips.

"You're Mary Wunderling. That's Coppertooth out yonder."

She nodded, rounding the corner of the bed and putting the water basin on a bedside stand.

"It's flattering to be remembered, Buck. I was a gangly-legged colt in pigtails the last time we met. At the Fourth of July dance in the Odd Fellows' Hall six years ago."

Temple closed his eyes, remembering what Jingo Paloo had told him about this girl who was already a legend in these hills. Orphaned by Indian attack, Mary Wunderling had chosen to remain on her parents' pre-emption claims, deaf to the offers of adoption from solicitous ranch wives up and down the range.

She was rubbing soapsuds into his beard, the touch of her firm finger tips filled with an electric soothing, when he asked:

"How long? Where did you find me?"

She worked up a lather with deft fingers, her head directly above his. "This is the sixth day since I found your horse standing over a gaping hole in a snowbank below the Grapevine. I don't know how long you'd been there. You were delirious then."

He picked that over in his mind, finding it hard to rationalize a week's elapsed time.

"How bad—Am I going to sack my saddle, Mary?"

The rangeland idiom touched off humorous highlights in her eyes as she reached in a pocket of her buckskin skirt and drew out a cased razor and strop.

"You won't die, Buck. Although there were times, a few nights back, when I thought I'd have another grave to dig down by the spring. You had a high fever."

The keen-whetted razor made easy going of his beard; he decided the razor must have belonged to her father, one-time Medical Corpsman in the Seventh Cavalry in the Dakotas.

"The sheriff?" he asked, dreading what news she might have for him concerning Brockway.

Mary toweled lather and hair from his left cheek and jaw, moving back to scrutinize her work with a critical eye.

"According to what Cap'n Collie heliographed me, Si Larbuck found Billy Winn's body and Canuck Brockway after one of the stage horses showed up at his corral. The last word from the Cap'n, the sheriff is still alive. He had both legs broken below the knee and a bullet in his right lung."

Temple had his moment of deep relief at this news. He felt fully responsible for what had happened at the Grapevine.

He felt better when Mary had finished shaving him; he wanted to talk, but the girl withdrew and he was asleep before she returned from watering the stock. Dusk had come to the mountain homestead when the girl roused him and spoon-fed him a nourishing beef gruel, hot and thick.

"I owe you my life if I pull through this," Temple said, when the contents of the soup bowl were gone. "I'm in your debt, Mary Wunderling."

She stood at the bedside, arms folded over her breasts.

"You owe me nothing. It is your horse that deserves your thanks. I was bringing in a haunch of venison when your pony whickered to my pinto, beyond a hedge of old ferns. He was standing vigil over you, Buck."

The girl went into the adjoining room and returned with a roll of boiled linen bandages. Watching her deft and graceful movements, Temple found himself struck by the comparison of this fully matured woman with the memory he had always had of "that little orphan down on the Wunderling place," the freckle-faced and elusive little waif of the rangeland whom he had occasionally seen riding up the Pass to town in years gone by, trailed by her brace of shaggy collie dogs.

"Time to change your dressings," she said, stripping back his blankets. "If infection sets in I'll have to call Doctor Kildenning down from Rimrock. I can do it by heliograph, so don't worry about being left alone."

This was Temple's first intimation as to the location or seriousness of his gunshot wound. For the first time, he became aware that his entire midriff was girdled with bandage; as they fell away under the deft snips of her surgical scissors, Temple glanced down to discern a stitched incision, four inches long, following the crease of his flesh below his short ribs.

"It looks like Doc Kildenning has already sewed me up."

Mary Wunderling shook her head, bending closer to inspect the condition of the flesh around the knotted sutures.

"I cut you open," she said casually, "so I

sewed you up. With thread from my sewing kit. I couldn't find any catgut in Daddy's kit."

Temple winced as the girl's fingers palpated the wound.

"You dug a bullet out of me, Mary?"

She turned the full strike of her green eyes on him.

"Of course. You wouldn't have survived if I hadn't. I couldn't wait for Kildenning. It was a race with gangrene."

His eyes ran wonderingly over her face, incredulous at the skill with which she bound fresh dressings around him.

"But, Mary, you can't be over eighteen," he protested. "To probe for a bullet in a man's carcass, extract it, sew up the wound afterward—that's a job for an experienced surgeon!"

Mary shrugged, arranging the blankets over his shoulders.

"My father was Custer's chief surgeon at Fort Lincoln," she reminded him. "I grew up in an atmosphere of scalpels and hemostats. I was only nine when I held the retractors while Daddy removed my mother's ruptured appendix by candlelight right in this room. Why shouldn't I know a few tricks?"

She left him with that miracle to ponder on; and it was full daylight again when he opened his eyes to find the girl waiting with his breakfast gruel.

"Why didn't you send for Doc Kildenning?" he asked.

"I wasn't sure you wanted anyone to know you were here. I wasn't sure what had happened down on the Grapevine."

He grinned, striving to understand this unmerited loyalty.

"You did right, Mary," he said finally. "I don't know who shot Winn and old Canuck. But I aim to find out."

When he had finished eating, Mary Wunderling smiled softly.

"Cap'n Collie signaled me this morning from town," she said. "The sheriff is safely past the crisis now."

Temple wanted to laugh, but the effort was too much for him.

"You're not only a skilled surgeon, Mary, but you carry on two-way communication across fifteen miles of thin air by Morse code. Cap'n Collie keeps you well supplied with the news of the outside world, doesn't he? Him and Jingo Paloo?"

She answered him from the outer room: "Cap'n Collie was a signalman with the Seventh Cavalry in the old days. And I think Daddy taught me the Morse code before I knew my ABC's. It's been a comfort, during snowbound winters, even if the Cap'n is too drunk most of the time to handle his mirror. And his spelling is utterly atrocious."

Buck Temple slept again, awakening at dusk to find the pony mail rider, Jingo Paloo, seated by his bedside.

"Call Mary a freckled little tike, would you?" chuckled the Texan, gripping Temple's hand. "She kept you from ridin' down the chute to hell, you old jughead."

Temple said, "She'll do to ride the river with, Jingo. How's Brockway making out?"

The laughter went out of Paloo's eyes. "He'll pull through," the mail rider said. "That's the trouble. He's too tough to kill."

Something in Paloo's inflection gave Temple his hint of worry crowding the Texan hard, quenching his bubbling good humor.

"Why, Jingo, we both love Canuck like a father. He's got to pull through."

Jingo Paloo glanced around at Mary; some signal must have passed between them, Temple sensed, for the girl said something about going out to feed the stock, and she slammed the outer door of the cabin for good measure.

"Jingo," Temple said, "what's roweling you?"

Paloo's shoulders lifted and fell. He said, "Mary thinks you're skookum enough to know. She didn't when I called here the day after she fished you out o' that snowbank."

Paloo reached in a pocket of his horsehide jacket and drew out a folded square of cardboard. Handing the placard to Temple, Paloo lighted the

104

brass lamp on the bedside table and turned up the wick so Temple could read the printed words.

$1,000 REWARD
will be paid in hand by the Mountain
Express Stage Line for the capture, dead
or alive, of
BUCK TEMPLE
aged 29, black hair, brown eyes, 6' 1",
180 lbs., lately of Broken Bit Ranch,
Cascade Co. Wanted for the murder of
William Winn, stage driver, and shooting
of the undersigned, at Grapevine Curve,
Coppertooth Pass, on Wednesday,
March 9, 1887. Information leading to
arrest of this man should be relayed to
JOHN BROCKWAY
Sheriff, Rimrock, W. T.

A giddy sensation forced Temple to squeeze hard on the reward dodger to keep from dropping it.

"My God," he whispered. "Of course old Canuck jumped to the conclusion it was my rifle that potted him. His back was turned, and Bill Winn didn't survive to tell the true story."

Jingo Paloo picked up the reward blazer and returned it to his pocket. His face was bleak as he said, "These bounty notices are strung all along the road from Rimrock to Yakima. Shoot on sight orders, Buck. What in hell is the true story?"

Buck Temple described what had happened at the Grapevine, knowing he could trust Paloo. He held back only the reason why he had rescued Jord Ramont, and the unsavory angle of the case which involved Avis Malloy's alibi for Ramont's whereabouts at the time of Karl Gothe's murder.

"Somebody besides me had figured to pull Ramont's fat out of the fire," Temple finished his narrative. "That's probably why Ramont was so brave in court, not trying to establish an alibi. He knew he'd be rescued before he reached Walla Walla."

"Any idea who shot you, lad?" Paloo wanted to know.

Temple scowled. "As a guess, I'd say those three riders were loggers in Ramont's crew. The big one with the rifle could have been that high-climber of his, Bull Corson. I'm not sure."

Jingo Paloo, his face grave and deep-rutted with concern, took a nervous turn up and down the room. Finally he wheeled to face the man in bed.

"Why," he demanded, "did you want to rescue Jord Ramont? After spreadin' the word among the ranchers that you aimed to fight his lumber outfit to the last ditch?"

Temple stared at the rafters, hating to be evasive with this man who was his closest friend.

"Ramont didn't murder Gothe. Don't ask me how I know."

Paloo hitched his thumbs in his shell belt, staring down at the Broken Bit puncher.

"I got more bad news for you, Buck. Jord Ramont ain't on the dodge. He's up in Rimrock right this minute, making his plans to start logging off Broken Bit's timber."

Temple sat bolt upright in bed, ignoring the stabbing of his bullet-torn tissues.

"Ramont in town? He hasn't been rearrested?"

Paloo shook his head. "It's like this, Buck," he said gently, knowing the shock his words would bring Temple. "Cap'n Collie got drunk right after the stage pulled out of town with Ramont last week. The old soak started braggin'. Said he'd perjured himself to get Ramont hung. When he sobered up the old scoundrel admitted he didn't know who really killed Gothe."

Temple sagged back in his blankets, his face drawn and white.

"Anyhow," Paloo went on, "Jord Ramont showed up in town two days after his getaway, bold as you please. Whoever did that shootin' at the Grapevine must have let Ramont know he was cleared of guilt in the Karl Gothe business."

Paloo came over to the bedside and gripped Temple's hand.

"Collie's known to be an irresponsible lunatic. He won't even go to jail for that false testimony he gave at Ramont's trial. The tough part of this, kid, is that Ramont has spread the word that it was you held up that stage, and that it was your Winchester that worked on Bill Winn and the sheriff."

Temple could only stare up at his friend, too stunned by Paloo's words to frame an answer.

"Ramont claims he run off to hide after seeing you make a getaway," Paloo went on. "Your Stetson, with your initials in the sweatband, was found by the road, and your trail leading off across the snowfield. The fact that you didn't visit the ranchers up and down the foothills, the fact you've been missing, was proof that Brockway couldn't ignore, son. That's why he finally issued that shoot on sight order for your capture."

The noise of Mary Wunderling's return to the other room was lost on Temple. He vaguely listened to Paloo's advice.

"Mary knows all this, kid. But as long as she's willin' to hide you out until you're shookum enough to ride, you got to hole up here. Nobody prowls around this homestead but me. On the outside, you'd get killed pronto by some bounty hunter."

Temple lifted his anguished gaze to Paloo.

"I want you to tell Canuck the truth about this."

"Uh-uh. Canuck Brockway ain't your good friend anymore, Buck. He's the sheriff of Cascade County, with his duty to do. He's got you pegged for Billy Winn's murder; the fact that he's crippled don't enter into it. You're a hunted outlaw, Buck. With a stiff price on your scalp. Outside of this cabin you're a dead man."

Chapter 8

Spring—overnight, it seemed to Buck Temple—spread a lush green carpet across the flat floor of the high park comprising the Wunderling homestead.

The ice went out of Arrowhead Creek one night, rousing him from recuperative slumber with its splintering thunder of released waters sluicing toward the Yakima and the sea. On the tenth morning after his arrival there, following days of rich warm rain, Mary Wunderling had a bouquet of fresh wildflowers in the heirloom bowl on the fireplace mantelshelf.

To Buck Temple, the healing of his punctured tissues seemed a slow, almost static thing; although when Mary had snipped her sutures and withdrawn them from his flesh she had showed her relief at the restorative powers of his body.

Spring meant a resumption of horse traffic along the game trails which girdled the base of Coppertooth Peak, and any passing rider might learn Temple's secret and move in to cash the bounty which Mountain Express had posted for his capture.

Mary, knowing that peril, had remedied one menace without consulting Temple: by night she had transferred his big blue roan stallion from her stable to a canyon pasture under the loom of Coppertooth, where its discovery by outsiders would be unlikely.

But the danger of his own position here was secondary to the jeopardy in which he placed this orphaned girl, whose short life had already had more than its share of tragedy. Temple made no secret of the fact that, as soon as he was able to ride, he was going to quit her homestead.

"I've got to let the sheriff know the real facts, Mary," he told the girl on the evening which marked his second week under her roof, and the first to find him sitting up in a Morris chair which had been brought by covered wagon from far-off Dakota. "Even if I wasn't the object of a manhunt, Mary, I couldn't stay here any longer. I wouldn't want to—"

The girl's face was obscure in the half-darkness of the firelit room as she caught up his trailed-off phrase. "You wouldn't want to compromise me. Is that what's wrong, Buck?"

This was not the first time Temple had found himself amazed at the maturity of this girl's speech. The bookcases on either side of the rustic fireplace were well-stocked with volumes of history and mathematics, grammar and literature; a full set of Shakespeare rubbed shoulders with the Major's tomes on various phases of military medicine.

This library, somehow incongruous in this

shake-roofed rock cabin in the wilds, undoubtedly accounted for Mary's well-rounded education; he could not recall the girl ever having attended the one-teacher school at Rimrock, the only school short of Ellensburg.

"Well," Temple responded, embarrassed by her candor, "you are a full-bloomed woman, Mary. And uncommonly pretty in the bargain. I don't intend to spend my life under the cloud of Brockway's manhunt, you know. Sooner or later this range will learn where I spent my convalescence. Tongues will wag. Forked tongues, especially the womenfolk's."

Mary Wunderling shrugged that off, as out of keeping with her naive, completely virginal philosophy of life.

"Let them talk. You have treated me like a gentleman. Which is a rare thing in this country where women are scarce, Buck. That was my father's only regret about coming to this uncurried range, so far from the finer things of life. He felt he wasn't being fair to me."

Temple thought, "She must know about me and Avis Malloy. I wonder if she knows that Jingo Paloo is in love with her?"

Long-lived forebears had bequeathed a virility to Buck Temple's bone and sinew which, augmented by Mary's nursing care, served to accelerate his convalescence now. Within the week he was able to dress himself and take short walks out of doors, always waiting for nightfall before leaving the cabin, in case bounty hunters might be scouting the homestead.

Every evidence of springtime about him added to Temple's restiveness, his impatience to confront Rimrock and make his peace with Canuck Brockway, before some bushwhacker's slug cut him down for the price on his head.

The approach of warm weather meant that Jord Ramont's logging crews had already moved into the timber at the end of Glacier Canyon; the ring of their axes had already sounded the knell of the cattle business in these foothills, at least so far as Broken Bit was concerned.

A sudden, unexplained cessation of the flow of Arrowhead Creek was a source of dismay to Mary Wunderling, when it came weeks in advance of the normal tapering of the spring runoff. Temple knew what had dried up that stream so suddenly.

"Ramont has thrown a dam across the head-waters of the Arrowhead, up on my ranch, Mary. To form a lake so they can build a head of water to float their cut logs down to a sawmill. He was waiting for the ice to break to finish his dam."

Midway through his third week of enforced idleness, Buck got the girl's permission to saddle her pinto one evening and, promising to dismount at any sign of internal stress on his wound, had a ride up to the back canyon where his own horse was fattening on the lush, fetlock-deep bluestem there.

The next night he carried his six gun on that excursion, and spent three hours in the moonlight practising his draw, sighting on targets, and dry-snapping the gun hammer.

The fever had wasted his muscles, taken the edge off his steady nerves; but daily, responding to the nourishing food which Mary Wunderling prepared for him from supplies brought in by Jingo Paloo, Temple felt the tone come back into his fibres, saw the slight hand-tremor diminish, approaching its former viselike steadiness.

The time came when he ventured out in broad daylight, keeping to the shelter of the round-about timber. Returning from his horseback trip, Temple reined up in the brush overlooking Arrowhead Creek, with the intention of scouting the open reaches of the homestead meadow to make sure no passing riders had dropped by the cabin.

Sitting his saddle thus, Temple's eye was drawn to a flash of white in the emerald depths of a deep pool at the foot of what had been a plunging waterfall before Ramont's dam had reduced the creek to a third of its usual runoff.

His first thought was that it was a swimming otter; then the white gleam surfaced in a roll of spume and Temple saw the wholly naked form of Mary Wunderling pull up on a jutting shelf of rock, shaking the water out of her tied-back hair, flexing the pristine beauty of her body like a nymph.

Unaware of her invaded privacy, the girl ascended the rocky slope opposite Temple's position, shafting sunlight putting sparkles on her rippling wet back. Reaching the crest of the rock ledge which formed the waterfall above the pool, the lacy cascade frothing about her ankles, Mary Wunderling posed for an instant like a statue chiseled out of flawless marble. Then she made her dive, cleaving the crystal surface of the deep pool with scarcely a splash.

Struck by a hot sense of guilt, Temple reined back into the brush while the girl was still submerged, doubled back and forded the creek at a point well beyond the girl's earshot.

Mary Wunderling's unspoiled loveliness and complete, primitive purity of soul and body made its warm inroad on the cowman's blood, seizing his full attention while he stabled the girl's pinto and filled the manger with cured clover hay.

She came in sight across the grassy park an hour later, pausing, as was her custom, to kneel for a solemn moment beside the twin mounds of her parents' graves, under the cottonwood which arched above the spring beyond the house.

Temple forced himself to meet the girl's eye as she rounded the cabin, to find him busy fitting a silver gun sight, fabricated out of a dime filed in half, on the barrel of the .45-70 Springfield rifle which he had removed from the elkhorn rack above the fireplace mantel.

"I've often wondered how you escaped that Indian raid, Mary," he said, mentioning her tragic past for the first time.

For answer, she led him into the front room, where she slept nights on the rustic sofa.

"I've told no one my secret about that," she said, and stooped to roll back a hooked rug from the puncheon floor. To the eye, the unbroken surface of those flattened logs revealed nothing unusual; but the girl removed one of the hickory pegs from its socket and a counterbalanced trap-door, four feet square, swiveled on its concealed pivots to expose the dark depths of a cellar beneath the cabin.

"The Indians overlooked this cellar," the girl said, sobered by the memory of that grim, long-ago catastrophe. "They got Daddy first, out by the woodpile; and Mama fell before she could reach his body. I was fourteen then. There was nothing left for me to do but slip through this trap and wait until the redskins left."

She closed the door and restored the hooked rug over it.

"It's been a handy hideout since," Mary said. "Drunken cowboys have visited this cabin, more than once, hunting for me. Thanks for putting that front sight on for me, Buck. That was Daddy's rifle."

The girl was preparing succulent strips of venison for their noontime meal when the dogs set up a clamor outside and Buck Temple moved across the room to a window, suspense putting its sharp edge against him. He saw a rider approaching from the direction of the Pass, the first visitor the homestead had known with the exception of Paloo's weekly appearances.

"It's Avis Malloy," Buck exclaimed, reading the quick alarm which Mary had shared with him. "The girl I aim to marry, Mary. It's all right for her to know I'm here."

Mary Wunderling pulled him abruptly away from the window, her eyes wide sprung with a nameless dread as they watched the former Rimrock schoolmarm put her gray stallion across the grassy flats at an easy canter. Avis was wearing a man's red shirt and a split doeskin riding skirt; her face was shadowed by the sweeping brim of a cream-colored Stetson that stood out sharply against the evergreen jungle behind her.

Every instinct in Buck Temple was aroused, crying out to send him to the doorway to call a glad greeting to the oncoming rider. But he found his path to the door blocked by Mary Wunderling, and panic was plain to read in her eyes as she faced him.

"Get into the cellar, Buck. For my sake. No one must know you're here. Especially a loose-tongued female."

Avis Malloy was only fifty yards away now; they could hear her melodic voice scolding the dogs which romped around her mount, filling the homestead with the echo of their barking.

"Mary, it's all right, I tell you. Avis—"

His hostess was already opening the floor trap. Looking up at Temple, her voice had a vibrant, pleading note.

"If you owe me any favor, Buck, do this for me. Your sweetheart never paid me a visit before. She doesn't like me. Please, Buck."

Because he was in this woman's debt, Buck Temple acquiesced to her unreasonable dread of his being discovered here, and descended into the dank root cellar by means of a pole ladder. The door swung shut overhead. Standing in the damp coolness, Buck could see the doorway up there through an interstice between two puncheons which the rug did not cover.

His ears registered the creak of saddle leather as Avis dismounted, close by the steps; he heard Mary Wunderling open the door to greet her visitor, and he caught Avis's reply:

"What a perfectly delightful setting, Mary! I envy you so. You're looking well, child. Why don't you ever come to town any more?"

Temple lost the exchange of banalities for

118

the time being; he quelled a desire to rap on the underside of the trap, knowing he could not violate Mary Wunderling's confidence.

Minutes later the two women came into the cabin; he heard the chime of Avis's spur rowels as she crossed the trapdoor inches from his head and seated herself on the horsehide divan.

"Mary, I'll be frank about my reason for coming here," Avis spoke in a controlled voice. "You must know that my fiancé, Buck Temple, disappeared almost a month ago after that shooting on the Pass road. I—I'm wondering if you have seen any trace of him or his blue roan in this vicinity?"

Mary Wunderling spoke promptly. "Your man must have left the Territory knowing the law is after him, Miss Malloy. You'll get a letter one of these days, postmarked faraway. Then you can go to him." She paused. "You would go to him, wouldn't you, Miss Malloy? You love him enough to share his life as an outlaw, don't you?"

Avis Malloy's laughter had a somehow brittle ring to it.

"What a suggestion, child! Of course, I'd go to Buck. Even though he killed a man in cold blood and very nearly killed Canuck Brockway, his best friend. Such things can't alter a woman's love."

Buck Temple felt a transcendent thrill stir him as Avis finished speaking. By that simple declaration of her faith and love, Avis Malloy had erased any disillusionment which recent events had put unbidden in the secret recesses of Buck Temple's heart.

He heard Avis get to her feet suddenly and cross over to the door entering his room.

"What a perfectly charming bedroom, Mary!" her voice reached Temple's indistinctly. "When are you going to let some lucky man share this idyllic existence with you?"

Avis Malloy made her polite good-byes a few moments later. But it was long after the beat of her pony's hoofs had been swallowed up by the timber beyond the meadow that Mary Wunderling released him from the cellar hideout.

"She took it upon herself to look into your room," Mary said angrily. "She was hunting for signs, Buck. I know it. And she found some. Your gunbelt, hanging beside the chiffonier."

Temple said miserably, "It's only natural she should be worried, not hearing from me, Mary."

The girl twisted away from his outreaching hands, her lips pressed thin. "I hate her," she said. "She is not worthy of your love, Buck."

A mile from the Wunderling cabin, where the encroaching pines grew broom-bristle thick to the edge of Coppertooth Pass road, Avis Malloy reined up her lathered stallion as a man pushed his horse out of the fernbrake to block the trail.

"Well?" Jord Ramont's single word revealed

the pressure of suspense that had ridden him during his vigil here.

Avis nodded. "Buck's hiding out somewhere on Mary's place. She disclaimed any knowledge of his whereabouts. But I saw his gunbelt hanging on the wall of Mary's bedroom."

Chapter 9

Up and dressed before the dawn's first light gilded his window next morning, Buck Temple knew with a pang of regret that this day must see his departure from Mary's roof.

Rapping on the partition door before entering the front room, the cowman got no answer. He found Mary's bedclothes already removed from the sofa and stowed away; the girl had fired the cookstove and coffee was boiling there, but he saw by the evidence of her dishes on the table that she had already eaten breakfast.

Going outside, he found no trace of Mary Wunderling at the barn or corral. Her pony was gone; her saddle was not on its accustomed peg.

Eating his solitary breakfast, Temple cleaned up the dishes and then took down the army-issue Springfield from the elkhorn rack. He knew where a four-prong buck and two does watered over on the creek near Blue's pasture; a replenishment of venison would help make up for the inroads he had put in Mary's larder during these past weeks.

He set out for the upper canyon on foot, shouldering the Springfield; and as he approached the edge of the timber he saw Mary Wunderling ride out of a game trail there, accompanied by her frolicking collies.

"Nice morning for a joy ride, Mary."

"I've been scouting the talus bench under the Peak. I've got something to show you, Buck."

The girl drew a knotted handkerchief from the breast pocket of her beaded buckskin jacket, and unfolded it to reveal a collection of miscellaneous objects—a burned stub of match, a cigarette butt, the tin label off a plug of Red Anvil chewing tobacco, a scrap of saddle thong.

"Somebody's been scouting the homestead from the high ledge, Buck," the girl said. "I've suspected it for several days now. It's a hard climb to that ledge. A man wouldn't go to that trouble unless he was sizing up the place."

Buck Temple nodded gravely.

"I'm leaving this morning, Mary. It has nothing to do with Avis's visit yesterday. I haven't felt any pain in my side for a week now. I'm lit and ready to ride."

Something like relief eased the tautness of the girl's facial muscles; relief tinged by a residue of sadness.

"I'll pack Dad's saddlebags with grub, and let you have his army canteen, Buck. You could reach the Canadian border on those rations, traveling by night."

Temple grinned up at the girl. "Making me hit the owlhoot, are you? Do you think I'd be happy away from this range, Mary?"

The girl stared down at him with a despairing hopelessness which was new for her.

"You'll be safe nowhere in Washington Territory, Buck. You have nothing to keep you around Rimrock. Broken Bit is gone. Even if Avis's father let you have it back, it'll be worthless by the time Ramont's loggers finish stripping the timber off your watershed."

"Somebody's got to fight Ramont, and keep him from spreading his operations, ruining other ranches."

She hurried on, ignoring him. "If Avis is the girl you think she is, she'll come when you send for her. Any girl would, if she loved a man."

Temple said gently, "You heard what Avis had to say about coming to me."

"She was lying. A woman knows such things."

They were skirting the fringes of a quarrel; Mary broke the tension by reining around and heading for the cabin.

Remembering the girl's sure evidence of spies covering this open ground from the ledge on Coppertooth, Temple hurried into the cool twilight of the game trail.

He had tarried too long to bag one of the muletails which watered in the Arrowhead pools. Finding his saddle where Mary had cached it in the fork of a twin hemlock, Temple cinched it on Blue and mounted.

The Morgan-Quarter horse, restive from nearly

a month's pasturage, had a skinful of steam this morning and the short bucking session served to convince Temple that he had made a complete recovery from his gunshot wound.

That feeling of well-being was welcome to the man; he had his further proof of his physical fitness when he kept Blue at a hard run all the way back to the meadow, feeling only the dullest of throbs in his belly when the saddle-pounding ride was over.

He unsaddled and turned the blue roan into the corral with Mary's pinto. He was heading for the cabin with the girl's Springfield when his eye was arrested by a blinding series of flashes from far up the cleft of Coppertooth Pass, in the direction of Rimrock.

"Cap'n Collie's heliograph," Temple muttered, hastening his pace to let Mary know that the old derelict was trying to establish contact with her.

He found the girl standing at the back door of the cabin, her eyes focused on the pulsing, intermittent glitter of the mirror which Cap'n Collie was manipulating from the ridge slope above Rimrock town.

He judged from the fact that the girl was already transcribing Collie's code message that she must have some prearranged time schedule for communicating with the old man.

A hand mirror was in Mary Wunderling's grasp

as Collie's remote flashes, fifteen miles away and two thousand feet higher up, broke off.

Standing at her back, Buck watched with a fascinated attention as he saw the girl carefully catch the sun's disk in her glass and align her return signals by means of two notched stakes nailed to tree trunks some distance from the cabin, sticks which had been carefully calibrated to conform with Captain Collie's line of vision.

Masking the mirror's flashings with her left hand, Mary Wunderling formed a brief string of dots and dashes. When she had finished her signaling, the girl slumped down on the doorside bench, her whole body trembling with a release of tension.

"Bad news, Mary?"

Temple's voice caused the girl to jump to her feet, as startled as if he had discharged a gun in her ear.

He apologized quickly. "Sorry. I know you concentrate pretty hard when you're heliographing. I thought you heard me come through the house just now."

Mary Wunderling flung herself against him then, her words spilling out, almost incoherent in their haste.

"Cap'n Collie says that Ramont and a posse of lynch riders left town just after daylight, headed down the Pass. Collie says they've got a line on your hiding out here, Buck."

Buck's arms closed about the girl, feeling the hard gusts of her breathing.

"Ramont must have trailed Avis down here yesterday, thinking she was meeting me here. I'm ready to ride, Mary."

The girl brought him the brand-new beaver Stetson which Jingo Paloo had purchased for him down in Yakima the week before.

"They've had time to get here by now," she cried. "Hurry."

Aware that her urgency was not without basis, Temple donned the new Stetson and hurried into his bedroom for his Colt and shell belt, putting them on as he followed Mary out to the corral. She was carrying a slicker roll of blankets and the saddlepouches.

Saddling up, he led Blue out of the corral, his eye fixed on the north rim of the timber from which Jord Ramont and his manhunters would most probably make their appearance on the Wunderling homestead.

As he lashed on the cantleroll and saddlebags, Mary Wunderling reached up to pull his head down to hers, kissing him on the cheek as a sister might.

It was their only intimacy up to now; Temple had a moment's wild longing to crush her in his arms, but he put the hot hunger in his blood aside, remembering Jingo Paloo's prior claim to this girl, and his own allegiance to Avis Malloy.

"Canada. Idaho. Go anywhere you think best, and God be with you, Buck," the girl panted. "But watch yourself on the way out. Ramont may split his riders and circle the bench before they close in on the cabin."

He stepped into saddle and would have leaned down to grip the girl's hand, but she was already sprinting for the cabin. He had often wondered what shape his farewell to this girl would take, and he regretted the abruptness of this parting; but time was fast running out on him and he roweled Blue into a fast getaway, heading straight for the nearest timber at the base of the Peak.

Bucking the underbrush, knowing he must avoid the open trails which might already be covered by Ramont's lynchmen, Temple next broke into the open on the crest of a ridge formed of alluvial talus eroded from the thousand-foot pinnacle of Coppertooth, rearing skyward at his back.

From this vantage point he had a view of the cabin and corrals at the edge of the wide park below, the details standing out in sharp clarity in this rarefied mountain air—the wisp of white smoke spiraling from Mary's chimney, her pinto rolling in the dust of the corral, the dogs cavorting out by the haybarn.

He glimpsed a blur of movement to the north, and swung his glance that way in time to see a file of horsemen break into the open and fan out, pounding across the meadow flats at a gallop.

Ramont's posse had missed him by minutes: Captain Collie's sun-flashed signal of warning from Rimrock had literally saved Temple's life.

The Broken Bit rider pulled up and dismounted, knowing he could not quit this vicinity until he was sure Mary Wunderling was in no way molested by these invading riders.

As if he were watching this scene through the wrong end of a telescope, Temple saw the lumberman's cavalcade make their wide, swift sweep of the homestead and close in from all angles, boxing the cabin and outbuildings.

Sunlight glinted on gun metal as that ring of steel constricted; Temple heard the clamor of barking dogs and shouting men, and saw, with a quick pang of dread, that Mary had left the cabin and was walking out to meet Ramont's lynchmen, the .45-70 Springfield slung across one elbow.

Even at this distance, Temple had no trouble recognizing Jord Ramont and his leggy Appaloosa. The lumberman appeared to be arguing with the girl; he saw Ramont signal his loggers to search the barn and sheds, while he and three of his henchmen dismounted and headed out of sight into the rock cabin, followed by Mary Wunderling.

Temple ground his teeth in futile suspense, visualizing the thorough ransacking that two-room cabin was undergoing. He saw the feverish search being made at the barn, saw hay being forked out of the gable opening as lynchmen probed the loft with pitchforks in search of their hidden victim.

After what seemed an eternity—by Temple's watch it was only an hour's elapsed time—Ramont and his men returned to saddle and headed off southward, to disappear under the rim of Arrowhead Creek's canyon.

An immeasurable relief flooded through Temple when he saw Mary Wunderling, apparently unharmed by the searchers, go out to inspect the shambles of her barn.

Temple decided to wait out this day, now that the sun was behind Coppertooth Peak. He knew the risk he ran of being spotted by riders Ramont may have deployed in the roundabout timber, and withdrew with Blue to a rocky defile forming one of the stumplike roots of Coppertooth Peak.

When full dark crawled down the Cascade slopes to westward, Buck Temple headed back down the steep knee of the Peak's base, knowing he could not leave without another word with Mary Wunderling.

Approaching the lamplighted cabin, the girl's dogs caught his scent on the wind and at their first outbreak of barking Mary Wunderling killed her light.

Temple identified himself with a cautious

halloo, and a moment later Mary joined him at the edge of the timber.

"Why are you back, Buck?"

"I had to know you were all right."

"They turned the house upside down looking for you," the girl said. "I'm afraid for what Ramont may do when he gets back to town. He may suspect that Cap'n Collie tipped you off with his heliograph."

Standing beside his horse, only an arm's length separating him from the woman, Buck Temple found himself unable to frame the words of gratitude he had so carefully rehearsed up on the ledge this afternoon.

"Mary," he blurted suddenly, "Jingo Paloo would make a good mate for you. He's young and ambitious. He was a top cowhand before he took on this mail riding contract. You have the makings of the best ranch in the foothills right here."

Under the stars, Temple saw the girl's cheeks take on a lively color, and he thought, "She's given Paloo some thought, then. That's a good sign."

Mary's reply was noncommittal. "Jingo is nice. Have you ever wondered why I stayed on here after the massacre, Buck?"

He made a vague gesture. "This homestead is as close to heaven as you're likely to get on this earth, Mary. Why should you have given it up?"

131

She stared off across the starlighted acres of her grassy expanse of benchland.

"I could run a thousand head of timber cattle on this land," she said. "I've even picked out my brand. A caduceus. Two serpents twined around a staff. The emblem of the Army Medical Corps that Dad devoted the better part of his life to, before he quit dragging Mother around from one post to another and struck down his permanent roots here. It took that wipeout from the Sioux on the Little Bighorn to accomplish that."

She glanced up to surprise his level scrutiny on her.

"Waiting for the right man to come along, Mary? You couldn't go wrong with Jingo Paloo."

"Jingo hasn't spoken for me, Buck. And I'll have to wait for '88 and leap year."

A night bird's sudden cry out in the far timber snapped Mary Wunderling back to reality; she said tensely, "Ramont may have left scouts behind on the off chance that you were hiding out in the timber. You must ride now, Buck."

Reluctantly, Temple readjusted his saddle girth and swung into stirrups.

"Then it's so long, Mary. I guess you know how much—how very much this little interlude has meant to me."

From the shadows he heard her soft whisper; "It's meant a lot to me, Buck. You know, you are the only boy who asked me for a dance that night of the dance in Rimrock."

And then she was gone, the swift strike of her steps fading as she hurried toward the darkened cabin.

The moon rammed a silver horn over the eastern desert, and by its glow, ten minutes later, Mary Wunderling had her last glimpse of Buck Temple, heading into the timber in the direction of Coppertooth Pass.

When he reached that outlet from the range, she assumed he would head east, on his way to the Canadian border, or south to Oregon, or perhaps across the Territory to the sanctuary of the Rockies.

But she had to know, and thus, before the moon was fully risen, she was saddling her pinto and following Buck's trail toward the Pass road.

Grapevine Curve was a twisting river of silver under the moon's rays when the buckskin-clad girl broke free of the timber and dismounted to search for Temple's sign in the dry dust of the road.

She saw where Temple had put his horse out on the road, at the identical spot where Ramont's gunhawks had cut him down from ambush a month ago. She saw where he had reined down-grade, following the ribbon of road that led to Ellensburg and the outside world of which she knew so little.

Then, clear as type on a printed page, the girl saw where Buck Temple had reversed direction and spurred Blue into a long lope, headed westward up the Pass toward Rimrock town.

Alone in this immensity of space and distance, Mary Wunderling let a little panicked cry escape her lips; and then she said aloud, "But of course Buck would go back and face the sheriff and the men who are out to destroy him. He wouldn't run away. Oh, ride with God tonight, Buck Temple. I love you so."

Chapter 10

Through the window at his bedside, Canuck Brockway had a view of the Timberline Saloon two blocks away, kerosene flares illuminating its weatherbeaten false front and the hitch rack reserved for the saloon's patrons.

The old sheriff's attention kept straying to that hitch rack now, as his old friend and neighbor, Doc Kildenning, explored the lawman's chest with the bell of his stethoscope.

"No more show of pink when you cough, Sheriff? Good. Tomorrow you can sit up in a wheelchair for an hour. You're a tough old buffalo, Canuck. Most of my customers don't survive a bullet in the lung."

This was news Brockway had been wanting to hear during the eternity he had spent in this bed, his legs sheathed from knees to ankles in grotesquely heavy plaster casts. But, watching Kildenning snap shut his black satchel and reach for his hat preparatory to leaving, the salty old Canadian had not heard a word the medico had said.

"You'll let me know first thing if Ramont's bunch bring him to your morgue, Doc?"

A patient wisdom showed behind Kildenning's steel-rimmed glasses. He laid a hand on the old lawman's arm.

"Hell, Buck Temple's too tough to be corralled, Canuck. And you're hoping against hope I'm right."

Brockway rolled his head despondently on the brace of pillows Aunt Molly had fluffed for him a few moments ago.

"I can't figger it, Doc. There was no reason to think Buck was hiding out in my county. Less call to think the Wunderling girl would hide him. It don't add up."

Doc Kildenning tarried to stoke his meerschaum with shaved plug. Ever since Ramont and his timberjacks had saddled up and left town this morning, dread had been gnawing at his patient's vitals, a strain that was tearing down the physical headway Canuck had made these past weeks. Worry could be as deadly as a bullet, sometimes.

"Ramont's got nothing but a wild rumor to go on, Sheriff. Now, you get some sleep, or I'll load you full of morphine."

Brockway closed his eyes; he heard Aunt Molly accompany the old doctor to the front door. Her voice drifted back.

"Buck was the closest thing Canuck ever had to a son, Doc. If Ramont brings him back, either way, it's going to go hard with him."

A rider galloped up to the sheriff's front gate as Kildenning was hobbling off through the night. Aunt Molly heard the hushed exchange of voices out there, and the prescience of disaster which had been building up in her throughout this suspenseful day became a tangible pain in her breast now.

She recognized the new arrival as Mose Hartley, her husband's deputy, and acting sheriff during Canuck's convalescence. She knew from the urgency of Mose Hartley's voice that he was giving Doc Kildenning some news concerning Buck Temple.

Hartley's boots made their abrasive grind on the pebbled walk as the deputy hurried up to where Aunt Molly waited in the doorway, her face strained and white.

"Relax, Aunt Molly," Hartley said gently. "Ramont's posse just rode in. They didn't flush Buck out of Mary Wunderling's place. The doc says it'll be good medicine to let Canuck know."

All the tension left the old lady at this news; which was a paradoxical thing, in view of her belief that Buck Temple's gun had cut down her husband.

After Hartley had left, Aunt Molly tiptoed into the old sheriff's room and found him asleep, a smile lurking under his sandy mustache. Blowing out the bedside lamp, she stood a moment staring through the window at the Timberline Saloon.

She saw the horses lining the rail in front of the deadfall, horses lathered from a daylong trek through the foothills, their jaded heads drooping to the gutter's dust. Ramont's riders, back from their abortive manhunt.

Aunt Molly found it difficult to analyze the sense of overwhelming relief which filled her now. A woman's heart couldn't make the change from love to hate overnight, no matter how impelling the motive; especially when Buck Temple occupied a corner of her heart second only to that reserved for her husband of forty years' standing.

When she had finished the supper dishes, Aunt Molly went into the parlor and opened her brassbound heirloom Bible to the Psalms, her favorite source of spiritual comfort. She was polishing her spectacles when she heard the jingle of a man's spurs coming up the front steps, followed by three clicks of the bronze knocker.

That was a cherished signal of other, happier times, that triple knock; it was the signal Buck Temple had used as a kid, when he had come to rummage through her cookie jar.

Aunt Molly stood frozen beside her Morris chair as the knock was repeated again. "It's a coincidence," she whispered, and hurried across the room to open the door.

Against the background of Main Street's lights, the man stood tall and motionless there, Stetson cuffed back over jet-black hair, hands thumb-hooked to the shell belt slanting across his tapered flanks.

"Buck!"

The sheriff's wife was weeping uncontrollably against Temple's shirt in the next moment.

"Aunt Molly, I didn't shoot Canuck. Can I see him?"

Stepping into the soft-lighted parlor, his eyes drinking in the myriad changeless details of the homey Victorian furniture and bric-a-brac which was the mode of the times, Buck waited until Aunt Molly had gone into the sheriff's bedroom to light a lamp and ease the shock Brockway might experience at this unexpected visitor.

Buck Temple walked slowly into the bedroom, reaching Aunt Molly's side before Canuck Brockway finally spoke.

"Come to give yourself up, boy?"

Temple reached down to grip his old friend's hand. Aunt Molly started to leave, but the cowpuncher reached out to encircle her waist with his free arm.

"I want you to hear this, Aunt Molly. Look, Canuck, I admit that was me wearing the mask, that day at the Grapevine. Why I wanted to rescue Ramont—I'll come to that. What you've got to believe, Canuck, is that the same gun that dropped you and killed Winn put this mark on me."

So saying, Temple jerked up the tail of his shirt to reveal the puckered, livid seam of a scalpel's scar on his hide.

Brockway's sunken features drew into a scowl. The scowl remained there while Buck Temple spoke briefly of his convalescence at Mary Wunderling's home.

"But you admit wanting to save Jord Ramont," the sheriff said dully, when Temple had finished accounting for his long absence. "In God's name, why?"

Temple sucked in a deep breath. "Because I had to keep Ramont from hanging for Karl Gothe's murder—a murder he didn't commit. I made my mistake not telling you that the night of the jury's verdict, but I—I thought it would complicate things. I thought I could play my cards so that Ramont would leave this country, and spare it a lot of bloodshed in the end."

He felt Aunt Molly stiffen inside the curve of his arm.

"Buck, are you trying to tell us it was you—"

He nodded grimly. "I killed Karl Gothe, Sheriff."

The sheriff closed his eyes. Finally he said, "Tell me about it, son."

"Well, I walked all the way up the Pass from Si Larbuck's that night, Canuck, because I couldn't wait another day to see Avis, and old Si had gone up the Greasy Grass to fetch my horse. I caught Gothe in the act of stomping old Collie to death in front of the Mercantile. I called him. Gothe pulled a gun, started shooting. I killed him in self-defense, Sheriff. The only life I ever took."

Aunt Molly and the sheriff remained mute, stunned by this revelation.

"I saw no reason to stick around town that night, Canuck," Temple went on. "I went back to Larbuck's through that blizzard, knowing Larbuck was away, that I had a foolproof alibi. You see why I had to give Ramont his chance at a getaway?"

For the first time, the gravity broke on Brockway's face. He propped himself up on one elbow and groped for Temple's hand.

"Maybe it's a trifle irregular, son, but I'm swallerin' your story for fact. Mebbe because I've loved you like the son God never blessed me with. Molly, run over to the office and tell Mose to come over. I'm canceling Buck's reward."

Buck Temple accompanied Aunt Molly to the door, and returned to the sheriff's bedside with grizzled old Cap'n Collie in tow.

"A witness to back my story, Canuck, along with Mary Wunderling. It goes without saying you won't prosecute Collie for perjury. He's irresponsible."

Collie eyed the sheriff like a boy caught in a jam jar.

"Yeah," he said, "I laid the blame on Jord. Knew it was Buck who shot Gothe, but I thought I could stave off a range war by cookin' Ramont's goose for 'im. Dang near did, too."

141

• • •

Deputy Sheriff Mose Hartley pushed through the batwings of the Timberline Saloon a half hour later. He paused there, fanning layers of sluggish blue smoke away from his nose with a sheaf of reward posters he had ripped from walls and fences up and down the cow town's length tonight.

Jord Ramont and his saddle-sore lumberjacks lined the bar, relaxing after their fruitless jaunt to Coppertooth Peak. They caught the grim clamp of Hartley's jaw reflected in the backbar glass, and knew the deputy had come here to get something explosive off his chest.

Hartley's appearance put an electric chill up and down the barroom, silencing the brittle laughter of the percentage girls, stilling the dry clatter of poker chips at the gaming tables, the nasal drone of the croupier at the roulette wheel.

That wheel's slowing revolutions measured the tapering off of all extra sound in this place; when the ball made its final bouncing click, Mose Hartley stalked across the sawdusted puncheons and, with every eye following him, reached up to jerk Buck Temple's dead-or-alive bounty poster from the walnut Ionic column which supported one end of the backbar cabinetwork.

"What's the idea of that, Mose?" the bartender asked in a startled half-whisper.

In the sepulchral silence which followed this

pregnant gesture of Hartley's, the deputy sheriff's drawled accents had all the impact of a bombshell on the ears of this saloon crowd.

"Ramont, you just got back from tryin' to smoke Buck Temple out of hiding. I'm letting you know that as of now, the sheriff is cancelin' out the bounty on Buck's topknot. We got evidence that Buck is an innocent man."

The utter stillness of the saloon was broken only by the sawing breaths of its patrons and the metronomic ticking of the fly-speckled clock over the street door.

To italicize his announcement, Deputy Sheriff Hartley proceeded to rip Temple's reward dodger into little squares and tossed the cardboard pieces into a spittoon.

The lawman was headed back across the barroom to leave the place when Jord Ramont broke the shackles of paralysis which Hartley's announcement had welded about him.

"Hold on, Hartley. It's no secret that Temple and the sheriff were thick as thieves before that business at the Grapevine. That don't mean Mountain Express won't pay off on Temple's hide if he ever shows up in Washington."

At the batwings, Mose Hartley turned slowly to put his drilling glance on the big lumberman.

"You think Temple's left the Territory? My friend, Buck Temple is back here in Rimrock this very minute. You two will meet up sooner or later. When you do, I'm warnin' you and your lynch mob to leave your irons in leather. Temple didn't shoot Winn. And he didn't shoot Canuck Brockway."

The slatted half-doors fanned on their unoiled hinges as the deputy sheriff stepped out into the night, leaving the Timberline as shaken as if Hartley had dropped a stick of dynamite behind him.

Ramont remained at the bar, fingers locked around a shot glass, one heel hooked on the rail. A drunken logger put a coin in the nickelodeon and the jangling melody of *Over the Waves* put its incongruous discord through the stunned quiet. A faro banker cursed loudly over the thumping of the music box and struck the instrument a splintering blow with the butt of a pool cue to silence its machinery.

Jord Ramont's eyes continued to stare at the fanning batwings where Hartley had disappeared. Lining the bar on either side of the lumber boss, Ramont's crew had lost color, a grim unease gripping every man in that group.

The Timberline was frozen in that tableau a moment later when the batwing doors pushed inward again and the tall, angular shape of Buck Temple moved into the glare of the ceiling lamps.

The big cowhand's face was shaded by the curved sweep of his Stetson brim, that shadow masking the lethal glint of Temple's amber eyes as his glance swung at once to cover the bull-shouldered figure of Jord Ramont.

This was their first meeting since the Grapevine episode; the drama of this moment put its chill across the barroom. Men edged away from Ramont's vicinity, trying to make their movements casual, but succeeding only in accenting their fear of gunplay soon to come.

Ramont's lips pressed firm beneath his close-cropped black mustache, a little bead of sweat making a rivulet along the ridge of his nose. Buck Temple moved a pace forward from the stirring doors at his back, arms loose at his sides, his right hand poised above and to one side of his gun butt.

"Ramont, you've had your chance to draw."

Temple's voice carried the restraint of a man whose temper was pushed dangerously close to the breaking point. Ramont's cheeks showed their bright spots of returning color as he carefully set his glass on the bar and unhooked his boot from the rail.

"I guess not, Temple." He lifted his two hands, the slight tremor in his splayed fingers there for all to see. "I'm tired from a hard day's ride. Give me another hour, and I'll match your speed and beat it."

At the left end of the bar, high-climber Bull Corson made a furtive jerk toward his thonged-down six-shooter. His big spatulate fingers had not brushed the notched stock of that .44 when Buck Temple's right hand dropped and lifted in the smooth, grooved draw he had practised so diligently these past days, and his cocked revolver came to a level covering of Ramont's lynch riders.

Somewhere in the back of the saloon a woman's scream broke with a frenzied pealing, ascending a treble scale until a man's fist slapped her silent.

Temple's gun kept its level warning over Corson's group as his eye ranged swiftly over the rest of the saloon crowd. Captain Collie was there, and Texas Sam Waterby of Diamond X; he heard Si Larbuck's cough outside the range of his vision to the left, and he knew he was facing a barroom crowd that was at least half on his side.

Ramont spoke carefully, "Pull your gun off my boys, Temple. Whatever brought you here is between the two of us."

Temple slipped his gun in holster.

"Peel down to the hide. Ramont," he ordered. "If you won't drag a gun, we'll see if you can keep me from smashing the living hell out of you with my fists."

Something like relief touched Jord Ramont's lips. He said in an amused voice, "I'll take that bet," and whipped off his ducking jumper and plaid shirt to reveal the hair-matted planes and ridges of a chest that had been deepened and hardened by a lifetime in the logging camps of the Northwest.

Tossing the garments on the bar behind him, Ramont unbuckled his gun harness and handed it to a pasty-faced bartender.

Captain Collie stepped out of the crowd to take Buck Temple's shirt and gunbelt; in the glare of the saloon's lamps the fresh purple scar on Temple's belly stood out like a whip's welt.

He thought, "I'm a fool to let Ramont bait me into a brawl while I'm out of condition," but he had made his challenge and it was too late to back out now.

Men began jostling away from gaming tables and the bar counter, to shape the edges of this impromptu arena.

As Ramont moved away from the bar, spitting on his palms and flexing his muscles in anticipation of the knockdown-drag-out brawl to come, Bull Corson saw his chance and, half drunk, made a second reach to gun butt.

He had his .44 half out of leather when a front windowpane was punched out by a rifle barrel, and Bull Corson found himself facing that rifle's bore.

Stepping out to meet Ramont, Buck Temple put his flicking side glance toward the window, and recognized that rifle resting on the sill. It was an army Springfield with a front sight fashioned from a silver dime.

Corson let his pistol drop back in holster as he realized that someone out on the saloon porch was siding Buck Temple, guaranteeing him against any treachery during his slugging match with Jord Ramont.

As Buck Temple stalked forward to meet the big lumberman's opening feint, one corner of his brain held its flaming thought: "Mary followed me here to back my play tonight."

Chapter 11

Ramont's haymaker was like a granite rock grazing Temple's jaw, as he parried the lumberman's plunging attack with a solid uppercut to the heart which rocked Ramont back on his heels.

Circling warily after that first jarring collision, both men lost all contact with the surrounding scene, blind to the close-packed ranks of bearded faces boxing them in, oblivious to the slippery sawdust underfoot. The hot glare of the shaded lamps overhead put their changing play of light and shadow over the rippling muscles of their stripped-down bodies. Physically, these two were an even match. Mentally, both men were primed to carry this fight to a killing finish.

Schooled in the rough-and-tumble tactics of barroom brawling through the long years he had spent in logging camps, Jord Ramont was entering this fight with the sole purpose of hammering Temple into bloody submission as quickly as possible, and then killing him with throttling fingers or skull-pulping kicks with his heavy hobnailed boots.

This murderous purpose was plain to read in Ramont's eyes as he feinted to throw Temple off guard and then rushed in from a side angle, attempting to pin his adversary against the bar counter.

Weathering that storm of hard-flung blows, Temple got squared around from the wooden barrier and back-tracked to make room for his own tactics. They were identical in weight and reach, these two giants; but Temple knew that a decision must come early in the fight. The recently-mended scar tissue in his belly would not permit this brawl to deteriorate into a prolonged struggle of attrition.

The ears of both men were unaware of the pandemonium about them, the hoarse calls welling from the collective throats of this rough crowd which jammed the Timberline from wall to wall.

These shouts grew to frenzied proportions as Ramont, chin hugged to chest like some grotesque bulldog, stalked after Temple's elusive shape with hard rights and lefts.

They met jarringly under the full glare of lights in midroom for a toe-to-toe exchange, Temple concentrating on Ramont's eyes and nose, the lumber boss striving to land a telling blow on the fresh bullet scar which he knew would be Temple's most vulnerable spot.

A smashing right hook broke through the cowman's guard and brought a gasp of sheer agony from him as Ramont's knuckles made their solid impact on his gunshot scar. He gave ground, white heat lacing through his torso, knowing a repeat punch would finish him; he felt himself falling as his spurs were trapped in a rolling cuspidor underfoot.

Ramont, diving in to press his advantage, came astraddle of Temple's falling body and his fingers clamped like the jaws of a trap over the cowpuncher's neck. Thumbs hooked like iron spikes into Temple's flesh as Ramont made his thrusting quest for the windpipe.

Ramont's bared teeth and flaring nostrils were obscure in Temple's eyes, behind a red curtain of pain which doubled momentarily as those throttling hands closed off his air.

He felt his senses teetering at the edge of black oblivion. Ramont's pinioning elbows were vise-tight as, sick and despairing, Temple clawed his arms free and concentrated his flagging energies on breaking the trap of the lumber boss' knees girdling his midriff, keeping his back to the floor.

Temple got a leg free and sent one spurred heel chopping against Ramont's head, a rowel raking its parallel gashes across the man's cheekbone.

Blood was a spattering warmth over Temple's face; its viscid slipperiness helped break the lumberman's strangle hold on his throat and as he felt Ramont's nails razoring ribbons of skin from his neck he jerked free and drove a following kick to the bridge of Ramont's nose.

There was a crimson curtain hiding the lower

part of Ramont's face as the two men broke apart and climbed to their feet, each bracing himself for the next phase of this savage meeting.

Ramont swung and missed with a left which would have blanked out Temple's ebbing senses had it landed; his own momentum cost Ramont his balance and Temple's partisans in the saloon throng screamed for the kill as Ramont went down on one knee.

But Temple's spent forces were unequal to the opportunity thus offered; he was too busy sucking oxygen back into his tortured lungs to keep Ramont down.

Temple had his kaleidoscopic glimpse of the round about crowd, the cleared gap in that group testifying to the presence of Mary Wunderling's rifle covering the loggers from the broken window.

Ramont's hairy forearm smeared red as he dragged his wrist along his blood-founting nostrils and expelled a slaver of froth from bruised lips, coming slowly to his feet with a grinding effort which told the crowd that Ramont was the first to show signs of tiring.

It was Ramont who gave ground now, backing away as Buck Temple made his approaching feint, searching for an opening through the big lumberman's defense.

The quick sidling put Ramont alongside the bar; the sheen of reflected lamplight on his whisky bottle caught Ramont's eye and the big man's right fist shot out to clamp around the neck of the bottle.

Temple's backers in the crowd roared their anger at this first sign of Ramont resorting to weapons other than his fists. Temple, knowing how quickly a bludgeon could end this fight, plunged in fast under the down-clubbing arm, felt the bottle shatter on his shoulder to leave a numbing ache down the entire length of his left arm.

He jabbed an elbow into the bloody ruin of Ramont's nose, felt the warm spray of following blood as he danced out of reach of the jagged bottleneck with which Ramont was now raking the air with back-and-forth arcs.

Ramont, concentrating on dragging that lethal handful of fractured glass across Temple's face, neglected to shield his own body with his other arm. Temple's incoming leap carried him away from the broken bottle and he drove a bone-splintering haymaker to Ramont's short ribs, all the weight of his swiveling hulk behind the blow.

He saw Ramont's bloody face go soft and limp as the punch drove the air out of his lungs. Ramont's arms came down from their own dead weight and Temple's hard kick sent the bottle-neck flying from Ramont's fist to shatter an overhead lamp.

The yelling crowd recoiled as Ramont plunged

backwards along the bar, warding off Temple's pursuing rain of blows with his elbows and forearms.

The shifting scene of battle carried Ramont hard against an overturned croupier's stool. Ramont snatched up that handy furniture, bawling deep in his throat like a wounded animal as he lifted the stool above his head and braced his legs to put leverage behind the downward sweep of his bludgeon.

Temple's feet skidded on the loose sawdust as he attempted to avoid the down-swinging stool. Hickory spindles splintered over his head and shoulders, seeming to jar his brain loose in his skull.

He fell forward against Ramont's legs and pulled the lumber boss to the floor. Locked in a grapple, they rolled back to the center of the barroom arena.

From scalp to heels, Buck Temple felt the numbing drag of his bruised flesh. Blood was a saline taste in his mouth as Ramont's fists clubbed his face, thumbs stabbing in gouging thrusts at his eyeballs.

They broke apart and moved back, lungs heaving, each fighter near the limit of his physical powers and knowing it.

Shaking blood from his eyes, Temple saw Ramont aim a kick at his crotch, his shoulders braced against the curved rim of the bar. Temple took that kick off his right hip, swiveling with it, and caught Ramont's leg with both hands when it reached the top of its arc.

Hauling backward with all his strength, Temple pulled Ramont off balance. Releasing the man's leg, Temple drove a right uppercut to Ramont's exposed jaw.

Temple's ebbing surge of strength was behind that blow; it was the big cowpuncher's last try, and the crowd knew it.

But the punch was enough to settle the issue. Ramont went down like a sledged beef, his eyes half open and glazed behind their film of blood. A fractured tooth dangled from his swollen upper lip like a stub of a cigarette.

Circling the fallen man, Temple knew it was over.

He reached down to seize Ramont by the armpits and pulled him to a seated position, his shoulders propped against the bar. He knew by the way the man's broken body settled when he let go that Ramont was out cold, punished beyond his capacity for punishment.

For the first time, the roar of the saloon mob reached Temple with an intelligible meaning. His friends were howling for him to kill this man—as Ramont would have done had the situation been reversed.

Instead, Buck Temple turned his back on the blood-drenched hulk, knowing by what a perilously thin margin he had escaped being down there instead.

Old Captain Collie's skinny shape hobbled into the hazy focus of his vision, fetching him his shirt and gun harness and Stetson.

"This ruckus," the old drunkard told the barroom at large, "is finished. Any doubts who is the bull of this herd?"

Shucking into his clothes, gun settled back in place on his flank, Buck Temple was vaguely aware of Captain Collie putting a bottle of bourbon into his hands.

Temple downed a fiery gulp of the liquor to steady his fainting senses. Then he smashed the neck of the bottle against the bar and sloshed the remaining whisky over Jord Ramont's face.

Coming out of it with the stinging fire of the alcohol lancing his wounds, Ramont glared dazedly about him, utterly spent, beyond any coordination. Through the pounding din in his skull, Ramont caught Temple's hoarse words.

"I got something I want this town to hear, Ramont."

Ramont's head slumped; Temple turned to face Bull Corson and the other loggers, bunched in a group at the far end of the bar, aloof from the rest of this hostile crowd.

"You can tell Ramont," Temple husked out, "that he's not loggin' so much as a stick outside of Broken Bit this summer. Tell him that."

The Timberline crowd remained mute before the ringing ultimatum. They knew they had heard an outright declaration of war; the foothill cattlemen who stood to face ruin before the threat of Ramont's timber outfit had their spokesman in this bloody wreck of a man who, until an hour ago, had been a wanted fugitive with a price on his head.

If the brawl had accomplished nothing beyond a personal settlement between Temple and Ramont, it had established in the eyes of the town that these alien loggers were not facing an unopposed summer of pillage and timber looting.

At the far end of the bar, Bull Corson spoke for his faction, trying to put conviction in his words by the sheer bravado of his bull-deep roar:

"You licked the boss in fair fight here, my bucko. Tryin' to skeer us loggers out o' these hills is somethin' different. You can tell your cow-wranglin' neighbors they'll have a losin' fight on their hands if that's how things are to be."

A pair of burly loggers were helping Jord Ramont to his feet as Buck Temple turned his back on that scene and zigzagged his unsteady path toward the batwings.

Reaching the door, Temple noted vaguely that Mary Wunderling had withdrawn her Springfield from the punched out hole in the saloon window.

Stepping out into the cool laving currents of the night breeze, totally oblivious to the groups of men who were knotted in bunches before each window of the saloon, Buck Temple stepped down to the plank sidewalk.

He saw Mary Wunderling's buckskin-jacketed figure swinging her pinto away from the hitch rack, saw her head down the Coppertooth Pass road toward her homestead without so much as a backward glance.

Thrust in her saddle boot was the Springfield .45-70 that had held Ramont's bunch in check during the brief, punishing minutes just past.

The fight was pushed out of Buck Temple's head as he watched the girl ride out of town. He heard the receding drum roll of hoofs as Mary put her horse across the Arrowhead Creek bridge at the edge of town. In the far distance he could see the steady twinkle of light, remote as a star, marking the site of her homestead cabin against the black scarps of Coppertooth Peak.

He turned his head to stare up at the window of Avis Malloy's room in the Trail House.

There was nothing to prevent his crossing the street and going straight to the arms of the girl he loved.

Instead, he turned down-street toward the refuge of the sheriff's home, beaten sick to the core of his being.

He saw Hal Dikus of the Lazy D staring at him as he passed out of the range of the Timberline's torchlight; and was reminded that he did not have the solid backing of the cattlemen in this fight against Jord Ramont's timber company.

Dikus' voice reached him across the dark. "You bit off a bigger chunk than you can chew, tellin' Ramont you were goin' to drive him and his kind out of these hills, Buck. This fight didn't settle a thing."

Another cowman's brief comment touched Buck Temple before he slogged out of earshot of the saloon.

"It settled one thing, Hal. Buck Temple's got himself marked for a bushwhack bullet now, that's for shore."

Chapter 12

Sitting his horse at the edge of a flowering rhododendron thicket on the west rim of Glacier Canyon, Buck Temple knew a smouldering anger and a sense of despairing frustration as he viewed the changes which had come to his Broken Bit.

The ranch house of whipsawed lumber which he had helped his father build so long ago had been taken over by Jord Ramont's twenty-odd buckers and fallers. Their small cavy of saddle stock shared his corrals with the heavy Percherons used for snaking sawlogs out of the woods.

The face of Broken Bit had changed almost beyond recognition in other respects. The big south pasture comprising Gideon Temple's original preemption claim was now a lake, a hundred acres in extent, the backed-up waters of Arrowhead Creek. An earthwork and log dam had been flung across a narrow point of the creek's canyon, impounding the spring runoff from melting snows.

This lake would be the holding pond for Ramont's timber; it would provide the head of water necessary for sluicing Ramont's cut down-creek to a sawmill site outside the foothills, where wagon transport would be available to supply Pacific & Western with crossties and trestle material out on the central desert.

From the north, Temple could hear the steady ring of two-bitted axes as Ramont's crews worked the virgin timber of the canyon. At irregular intervals, the cowpuncher caught the clarion call of "Timber!" running down the breeze, followed by the splintering crash of some ponderosa pine, centuries old, hitting the earth with shuddering force.

"Timber!" Was that to be the swan song of Broken Bit, the beginning of the end for cattle raising as the Rimrock country knew it?

The smokes of donkey engines lifted from the timber yonder, engines which would snake immense logs, some five feet thick at the butt, into the creek for floating to this holding dam lake. Already, the surface of that shallow pond was nearly covered with untold thousands of feet of cut logs. It would be but a matter of days before Ramont would open his floodgates and send his first consignment of timber down the Arrowhead to his mill site.

This was the fruition of a tangled pattern of events which had had their start in Temple's arrest for murder last fall, in trader Karl Gothe's buying out Broken Bit with money undoubtedly furnished him by Ramont, and with Gothe's subsequent resale of the ranch and its subsidiary timber rights to Genesee Malloy.

This Glacier Canyon was like a root, tapping the unsurveyed millions of acres of government timber which mantled this slope of the Cascades. If Ramont's crews stripped those hills of their sheltering trees in the months and years to come, erosion and drought would spell the ruin of cattle raising here for all time.

And thus far, Buck Temple was the only cattleman with the savvy to read the handwriting on the wall and offer Ramont even as much as a threat of opposition to this rapine of the Rimrock country's most precious natural resource.

Sick to the core, Temple reined his blue stallion back into the fern-bordered game trace which had brought him here from Rimrock this morning, and headed south toward the cow town. A week had elapsed since his meeting with Jord Ramont at the Timberline Saloon; the scars of that fight were still healing, his face a cartoon of mottled greenish-purple bruises, his torso corseted with Doc Kildenning's layers of bandage, trussing broken ribs which would take weeks in the knitting.

He dipped down under the rim of Arrowhead Creek's canyon when he reached the drift fence which divided Broken Bit from Hal Dikus' Lazy D range. He was jogging along the wagon road his father had built up from Rimrock twenty years back, when he caught sight of Jord Ramont and Genesee Malloy horsebacking down a side road which led from Dikus' headquarters.

Temple put his roan behind a jungle of bushes, not trusting himself to avoid a shooting in the event of a face-to-face meeting with the two men who had already engineered his ruin as a cattleman.

He heard the muted conversation of the two riders as they passed him, heading north toward Broken Bit; and after the beats of their ponies' hoofs had thinned in the distance, Temple gigged his roan back into the open and struck Dikus' road at a gallop.

A ring of hammer on anvil directed Temple over to the Lazy D blacksmith shop, where he found the old rancher superintending the shoeing of a span of mules.

Dikus' cowpunchers, native to these foothills, and, therefore, old-time associates of Temple's, paused in their work to wave a greeting to the Broken Bit outcast. In response to Dikus' called invitation to light and cool his saddle, Temple shook his head and motioned for the old man to come out for a powwow beyond the earshot of his cowhands.

"What's on yore mind, Buck?"

Dikus' voice carried a thin veneer of hostility; this rancher had his back up, was on the defensive, knowing Temple could not have missed seeing Ramont and Malloy leaving Lazy D.

"Hobnobbing with your new neighbors up the creek, Hal?"

Dikus' leathery cheeks stained a mahogany hue, stung by the sarcasm in Temple's tone.

"Now, Buck, I got to live with my neighbors. I ain't sayin' I prefer Malloy to you, by a damn sight."

"What did Ramont come to see you about?"

Dikus bridled. "That's none of yore business, Buck."

"It's my business if you sell out your timber rights to Ramont. He could use Goose Creek Canyon to make another logging road back into the hills to tap that government timber. The only way to hold Ramont down is to deny him right of way to that timber."

Dikus chewed his waterfall mustache, anger bubbling in him.

"By God, I'll tell you what Ramont offered me. Ten thousand in cash for my timber, and a third of what the railroad pays him for lumber produced on Lazy D range."

Temple hooked a lanky knee over his saddle pommel and fished in his pocket for the makings.

"You accept the offer, Hal?"

"Told him I'd think it over. I think I will. Like I told you in town after Ramont's trial, nothin' can stop Ramont from goin' up into the hills after that timber nohow. I might as well cash in while I can."

Temple fired his cigarette, expelled twin forks of smoke from his nostrils.

"You got a contract with the Yakima Cattle Company to summer graze their beef, Hal. At a dollar a head. How much did you make off o' that contract last summer?"

"Around six thousand."

"Multiply that by ten and you estimate Lazy D's potential take for the next ten years. You know what will happen if Ramont turns your range into stumpland? Second growth brush will choke out your grass inside of two years, Hal. In one season Ramont's loggers can ruin what it's taken nature hundreds of years to build up. Think that over, before you sign Ramont's papers, my friend."

It was nearly sundown when Buck Temple got back to Rimrock. Because he felt he had imposed on Aunt Molly Brockway's hospitality too long, he headed into the Trail House dining room to order supper.

He was waiting for his order when Avis Malloy came into the dining room. This was their first meeting since that morning at the hotel stable when Temple had picked up Ramont's gelding; the girl had been away on a shopping trip to Seattle at the time of his brawl with Ramont in the Timberline Saloon.

Avis had left Rimrock the same morning that Ramont's lynch riders had left for Mary Wunderling's homestead, he had later learned.

There was a strained aloofness in the girl as she came over to Buck's table. He rose, meeting the challenging strike of her eyes; it was not the look he had hoped to see from the girl he planned to marry, reunited after his month's absence following the disaster at the Grapevine Curve.

"I must say I hardly expected to ever see you again, Buck."

The cowman's expression was deliberately blank.

"You see me now, Avis. Glad?"

She bit her lip. "The rumor has it that you hid out at the Wunderling girl's homestead after that stage holdup."

Anger flickered in Temple's agate eyes. "The rumor is true enough. Don't fall over yourself thanking me for pulling Ramont's bacon out of the fire, Avis."

She smiled crookedly. "I'm sorry about that. Jord wouldn't have hung anyway when Captain Collie's perjury became known."

Temple sat down. "All right," he said angrily, "we'll drop the subject. I'm damned if I can understand you, Avis."

She came around the table to stand at his side.

"Were you hiding at Mary's place the day I visited her?"

"I was. Did you know that Ramont's bounty hunters were watching that homestead, that your visit brought Ramont's bunch down to Coppertooth Peak hunting for me?"

Avis Malloy flushed, a slow fear kindling in her eyes. She reached out to touch a scabbed bruise on the angle of his jaw.

"Have you ever thought of the position you put me in, Buck—you and Mary Wunderling ganging up on Jord at that cheap saloon? Everywhere I turn, women stare at me and whisper behind their hands. They're saying I'm engaged to marry a cheap barroom rowdy."

Temple looked up sharply, eyes bitter, his patience stretched thin. "Are we still engaged, Avis?" he asked. "You're still considering being the wife of an ex-convict from Walla Walla?"

Avis bit her lip, knowing that he might be baiting her into saying the word that would end the secret sham of her betrothal to him. But burning her bridges behind her was not a facet of Avis's temperament; she was a born opportunist, adept at playing both ends against the middle, picking and choosing such friends and alliances as would gain her the most out of life.

"Buck," she said, her tone gentling, "I'm sorry. We mustn't quarrel this way. Come and see me when you've finished supper."

She turned her back to him and strode out of the dining room. Later, from her upstairs window, she saw Buck Temple leaving the Trail House. She saw old Si Larbuck of the S Bar L pull his horse over to the wooden curb for a word with Temple.

Larbuck's voice drifted up to Avis.

"Jingo Paloo done like I asked, Buck, spreadin' the word about the mass meetin' of the Cattlemen's Association. I got bad news for you."

She saw Temple's head jerk up. "So?"

Larbuck spat into the dust, piling his gnarled hands on saddle horn.

"So far, Tex Waterby and Joe Redwine are the only outfits that have signified any notion of attendin' that meetin', son. The others made fishy excuses to Jingo. The way it stacks up, Ramont's got these foothills on a downhill pull. The ranchers are afraid to buck him."

Buck Temple's big shoulders went slack.

"I ought to let 'em go to hell, Si. Broken Bit's already on the skids. But I got an ace up my sleeve."

Larbuck eyed his friend quizzically. "That wasn't tall talk, then, what you told Ramont's gang at the Timberline last week? You aim to fight him to the finish lonehanded?"

Avis saw Temple's Stetson bob to the emphasis of his reply.

"Ramont's not got much time to make good on his contract with that railroad. Jingo Paloo tells me a rival outfit is biddin' with P & W to furnish lumber from the Okanogan country. I aim to break Ramont, Si. And that's not just talk."

Later, watching Temple ride out of town, bound eastward along the Pass grade, Avis Malloy thought with a jealous fire stirring through her, "Buck's going down to spend some more time with that Wunderling trollop."

Two days later Rimrock's populace gathered at the Arrowhead Creek bridge to see Jord Ramont's first head of water come plunging down the gorge, waters released from the control gates of his dam at Broken Bit ranch.

Riding that rushing flood were the first logs intended for the sawmill Ramont had set up at the foot of the mountains, within easy hauling distance of the railroad right of way in the eastern desert.

Following the vanguard of those racing logs, on horseback, were Ramont and his husky crew, armed with peaveys and block and tackle equipment to use in breaking up potential log jams further downstream.

It was the next morning that the boss at Ramont's mill flashed word by telegraph that the consignment of timber had failed to reach the mill on schedule. That news meant a serious log jam somewhere along the creek; it sent Ramont riding down Arrowhead Canyon to locate the cause of the stoppage.

He found it where the creek made its wide bend

to avoid the upthrust of Coppertooth Peak, fifteen miles below Rimrock.

A vast avalanche of boulders and alluvial earth had spilled down from the base of the lava rock spire, to block the creek's gorge from rim to rim under untold thousands of tons of fractured rock.

The loose boulders permitted the river's flow to filter through the barrier, but jammed against the upstream face of the rock slide Ramont discovered the splintered logs he had sent down from Broken Bit, the sum total of a month's work in the woods by his crew.

Thousands of board feet of potential lumber were piled up in a spectacular jam like straws in a haystack, a disaster without parallel in Ramont's experience as a lumberman.

Staring aghast at that mighty blockade of rock and earth, reading the doom of his own connivings in this calamity, Ramont turned to Bull Corson, the beefy-chested high-climber who had made the scout down the canyon with him.

"It must have taken an earthquake to have started that avalanche, Bull. You realize what this means? We couldn't blast through that slide in six weeks. This plays hell with our fast and cheap transportation to the mill yard. This means we've got to haul our cut outside by wagon or lose our P & W contract to our Okanogan competition."

Corson spat over the rimrock and said succinctly, "No earthquake, boss. There's the source of your trouble, ridin' out of the brush over yonder."

Ramont swung around, staring across the blocked-up creek to see the tall shape of Buck Temple spurring his blue roan saddler out of a jungle of wild huckleberry brush on the opposite bank. A Winchester carbine was slanting across the swellfork pommel of the Broken Bit rancher's saddle as he drew rein, facing the two lumbermen across the twenty-yard gulf.

"You back of this avalanche, Temple?" Ramont shouted above the gurgling, draining roar of the creek's flow through the rocks below the splintered logs.

The Broken Bit man nodded, sitting tall and confident in saddle, thoroughly enjoying this moment.

"A couple of cases of dynamite planted in the right place has paid back part of my debt to you, Ramont."

Ramont could only stare, his senses reeling under the impact of the cowpuncher's words.

"You see," Temple shouted, "you neglected to get permission from the downstream owners of Arrowhead Creek to float your cut over their property, Ramont. Right now you're on Mary Wunderling's homestead. She controls half a mile of this creek."

Ramont sagged in the saddle, his own violent impulses held in check by the threat of the

171

Winchester held so carelessly across Temple's pommel.

"As long as I'm doing all the talking," Temple went on, "I might as well tell you you won't be using Arrowhead to float your cut to the mill—not this summer, or next. And don't get any fancy ideas about blasting through this dam of mine. I'll shoot the first man I see prowlin' around this part of the canyon, night or day from here on out. I got nothin' else to do."

Ramont reined his Appaloosa gelding around with a savage jerk at his reins, crowding Bull Corson's horse off the trail.

"You win this round, Temple," Ramont's answering shout echoed off the fluted scarps of Coppertooth Peak. "I wouldn't make any bets about how long you'll keep me shut off o' this creek, if I were you."

Temple's cold laugh followed Ramont and his high-climber as they headed off up the canyon, soon lost in the perpetual twilight of this conifer-screened gorge.

Chapter 13

News of Buck Temple's spectacular one-man blockade of Arrowhead Creek had its profound repercussions in Rimrock and the outlying cattle country.

With a contract deadline to meet with the desert railroad, Jord Ramont had staked everything on the cheap and rapid method of transporting his cut timber to his sawmill by means of the waterway which linked Broken Bit with the outside world.

Temple, by the adroit use of dynamite, had dealt Ramont's lifeline a crippling blow. Foothill ranchers, pondering the lumber company's proposals for buying out timber rights on their range, now took fresh heart and stalled off making final decisions until they knew the final outcome of Buck Temple's coup.

In Rimrock, the burning question occupying the minds and hearts of its populace was "How long can Temple hold the fort? How long before Ramont blasts his way through that rock jam?"

Vague rumors drifted back to the cow town. Buck Temple, it was said, had stationed himself on a high ledge of Coppertooth Peak with Winchester and field-glasses, making his one-man defense of the stretch of Arrowhead Creek which he had blockaded against Ramont's logs.

Three days after Ramont's discovery of the Coppertooth Peak dam, the sounds of gunnery had echoed across the pine-clad hills in the vicinity of Buck Temple's guard post. Ramont, converging his men at Coppertooth Peak, had been unable to smoke out the lone cowpuncher hidden in the talus boulders. In fact, so the rumors ran at saloon bars and Main Street porches, two of Jord Ramont's loggers now occupied unmarked graves somewhere in the tangled upfling of ravines and ridges within range of Buck Temple's .30-30.

Rumors these might be; but Deputy Sheriff Mose Hartley, paying a visit to the Wunderling homestead, brought back a report of having talked to Buck Temple in person. Ramont had made his assault and failed.

"Buck's fightin' our battle for us," Si Larbuck of the S Bar L spread on Greasy Grass Creek informed the town. "Any man who sells his timber to Ramont this summer is a damned fool and worse; he's a traitor to the whole range."

April brought its hot days and cool nights, and heavy rains filled Arrowhead Creek with its thunder of racing white waters once more. That covering sound caused Buck Temple to increase his vigilance, especially after dark; he knew what opening this canyon meant to Jord Ramont, and he knew how effective a few charges of dynamite could be in clearing out his blockade.

Bellied down on the wet rocks of his lookout ledge, Buck Temple's sharp-tuned ears caught a muffled thud of hoofs on rubble on this April night following a seasonal rain. His slicker made its rustling sound as he reached for his carbine and levered a cartridge into the breech; his eyes raked the white boiling of the waters which dashed their spume over Jord Ramont's jumble of shattered logs on the upstream side of the blockade, searching for the blur of movement which would locate that rider.

A shift in the wind told him the horseman was approaching from the downstream side of the dam; he swung his Winchester that direction and laid a warning shot through the trees at the base of the peak.

Coming from that direction, the rider might be Mary Wunderling, who supplied him with grub and ammunition every other day. But the homestead girl had strict instructions to visit his guard post only in full daylight, and to send her halloo well in advance of her coming.

"Hold yore trigger up there, Buck!" a voice drifted up the talus slope, close on the heels of the racketing echoes of the shot. "I got news for you."

It was Jingo Paloo; except for a brief visit from Si Larbuck two days ago, this was Temple's first contact with how things were going outside.

"Leave your bronc and hoof it," Temple called back to the unseen Texan in the brush below his lookout. "You took a risk, son, not singing out before you did."

Jingo Paloo's lanky shape came in view, silhouetted against the creaming foam of the creek's rain-swollen runoff in the canyon below. The pony mail rider halted at the foot of the talus, peering up at the black overloom of Coppertooth.

"No need skinnin' myself up comin' to see you, Buck," the Texan called jauntily. "You can come down offen yore perch, you damn billy goat. Ramont's pulled in his horns. He won't be molestin' your dam."

Temple got to his feet, leaning on the grounded butt of his rifle, his shape still invisible to Paloo.

"What's the deal, Jingo?"

Paloo struck a match, lighting a cigar behind cupped fingers.

"Jord Ramont's movin' his lumber out with wagons, kid. I passed fifteen-twenty big Conestoga loads of crossties comin' down the Pass grade this afternoon."

Temple pondered this news momentarily, feeling the quickening tempo of his pulses. If Paloo was giving him a right steer, this could only mean that Ramont had given up all hopes of reopening Arrowhead Creek.

"Could be a blind to make me pull off my guard," Temple called back suspiciously. "Hey, you say those wagons were loaded with crossties, not logs?"

He saw Jingo Paloo nod.

"Sawed stuff, son. Dimension lumber, ties. You see, Ramont brung his sawmill up to Broken Bit three-four days ago. Dismantled, so nobody knew what his wagons were bringin' in."

Temple found himself grinning for the first time since this two-week-old ordeal of guard duty had begun.

If Ramont had moved his mill into the mountains, away from the lower end of Arrowhead Creek, it was proof positive that the lumber boss had given up any plan to float his cut out of the foothills. The expense and difficulty of dismantling his mill and transporting it fifty miles into the Coppertooth Pass country was too gigantic an undertaking to be brushed off as a mere bluff to draw Temple away from his blockade.

"Be right with you, son," Buck called down to his friend. "Got to roll my soogans and pack my gear out of here."

Quitting this lofty vigil on Coppertooth's ledge was a welcome relief to the Broken Bit puncher; he had felt imprisoned during every nerve-taut hour of his self-imposed duty here.

Joining Paloo on the creek's rim, Temple was in rare good spirits as they loaded his bedding and other equipment on Paloo's waiting horse.

"Ramont will play hell meeting his contract with P & W now," Paloo chuckled, slapping Temple on the back. "He'd need a thousand wagons to keep his lumber movin' from the mill to the desert. The foothill ranchers ought to vote you a pension for life for savin' their bacon."

Mary Wunderling was waiting for them at her cabin. She had taken care of Temple's blue roan during his stint of guard duty up on the Peak; in her eyes tonight was a fierce pride in his achievement which touched off a strange torment of longing in the cowman's heart.

"You know, Mary, I've been too busy to thank you for backing my play at the Timberline that night. You shouldn't have followed me to town like you did."

The girl caught Jingo Paloo's sharp interest, and something in the mail rider's look caused her to avert her eyes.

"And you shouldn't have returned to Rimrock, Buck. I have a feeling Ramont will never rest until he sees you dead. What are you going to do now?"

Temple tugged his lower lip thoughtfully.

"The outfits must be working on their calf round-up now. The Association has got to move its young stuff up to Skyline Flats before the big herds come up from the desert to use their summer graze. Reckon I'll brace Si Larbuck for a job."

Paloo nodded. "Larbuck's already hazed his little jag of S Bar L stuff up to the holding range above Dikus' place. His spread was deserted when I came by this afternoon."

Temple's brows lifted in surprise. The progress of the foothill calf gather showed how completely out of touch he had been with local events during his hitch at the Peak.

"Then I guess I'll rattle my hocks up to town tonight," Temple said, donning his Stetson, "and spread my blankets at Brockway's."

Paloo, reading the thought in his friend's head, said casually, "You won't find Avis at the hotel. Her and old Genesee have moved up to Broken Bit for the summer. Looks like it'll be a mite embarrassin' to visit your girl, now that she's roostin' in Ramont's camp."

Temple, building a cigarette, avoided the gaze of these two.

"Let's ride," he said to Paloo. "We can't keep Mary up till all hours this way. And thanks for playin' nursemaid to my horse all this time, Mary."

The girl met him at the door of the cabin, her big eyes shadowed with secret doubts.

"Buck, you'll take care of yourself? You know how Ramont will feel, after what happened at the Timberline that night, and your blocking the creek on top of it."

Temple grinned. "The only thing I've ever let

worry me," he said, "was what Ramont might try to do to you in retaliation for letting me put my blockade across the canyon on your land."

Rimrock's saloons were ablaze with light at one-thirty when Temple and Jingo Paloo cantered into the town's outskirts. Paloo made his headquarters in a lean-to behind the Mountain Express office at this end of his mailrun; he left Temple in front of the sheriff's cottage, where a light burning in the window indicated that the Brockways had not yet retired.

"You better bear in mind Mary's warning, Buck," the Texan said gravely. "Ramont won't rest easy until he's squared his accounts with you. You been crowdin' your luck perty steep since you got back. Yore back ain't bulletproof, you know."

Dismounting at Brockway's gate, Buck Temple regarded his friend for a long moment, choosing the words he had to speak to this man.

"Jingo, what's to keep you from asking Mary? She can't go on runnin' that homestead by herself, making her living raising garden truck like she is. The best spread of grass in the foothills is goin' to waste for want of a man to help stock her range."

Paloo's bantering good humor was erased from his puckish face in an instant.

"Mebbe," he said, "I'm holdin' off because Mary's got her heart set on another hombre. How blind can a man be, amigo?"

Paloo curvetted his pony away from the sheriff's fence and was gone in a boil of dust.

The Texan's words put a disturbing unease through Temple, the feeling persisting during the time it took him to turn Blue into the sheriff's corral.

Entering the house with his bedroll over his shoulder, Temple found the old sheriff seated in a wheelchair in the front room, the casts now removed from his legs.

"Back from doin' a big job for a bunch of ungrateful neighbors, eh, Buck?" was Brockway's greeting as they shook hands. "If I was able to ride, son, be damned if I'd let you out of my sight as long as Ramont is hangin' around."

Temple grinned bleakly. "I don't think Ramont will last long in these hills," he said, "trying to keep up with his railroad contract with a string of mudwagons."

Temple left Rimrock the following morning, heading for the heart of the hills where the Arrowhead Creek ranchers were busy with their annual chore of chousing their young stuff out of the timber for branding.

Temple, lending his services to whatever chuckwagon camp happened to need his rope and peg pony most, worked his way during the following week for forty-odd miles north of Coppertooth Pass.

This was the first spring in nearly twenty years that the Broken Bit branding irons remained unheated. Passing his former spread, Temple saw that Jord Ramont's sawmill was in operation around the clock, as the lumberman made his desperate effort to make up for the loss of timber he had suffered in the Arrowhead Creek debacle.

Already, a good half of the prime stand of ponderosa in Glacier Canyon had been logged off, stripping the once fertile timber-cattle range to a bleak expanse of stumps and slash piles.

Coppertooth Pass, leading out of the mountains, was choked twenty-four hours a day with Conestoga caravans, loaded to capacity with cut lumber on outbound hauls, returning empty for reloading at Ramont's mill on the Broken Bit.

These days, witnessing the wanton spoilage of his home ranch, found Buck Temple in saddle throughout the daylight hours. It was tough work, chousing stock out of the myriad gulches and meadows. Along a fifty-mile frontage, the smokes of branding iron fires lifted into the late April sky; fires tended with the utmost vigilance, for these timber-cattle ranchmen knew the menace which an uncontrolled forest fire could bring to their lands.

Temple's hands toughened their layers of calluses as he wielded lariat and branding iron hour on hour, day on day, moving from ranch to ranch as the calf gather neared completion.

Because these small tally outfits depended for their main revenue on leasing summer range to the big Yakima and Ellensburg syndicates, it was their custom to run their own stock to the higher mountain meadows west of timberline, leaving the more readily accessible graze of their own holdings for the use of the outside outfits.

This yearly procedure entailed minor cattle drives, once the calf crop had been branded; Association members pooling their herds, cutting out their individual brands at the big fall round-up prior to the main drive west of the Cascades to the slaughterhouses on Puget Sound.

Buck Temple found himself riding for Tex Waterby's big Diamond X spread when the foot-hill ranchers converged their steers, she-stock and young stuff on the high meadows above the Lazy D, known as the Skyline Flats.

Throughout the summer to come, each rancher would assign reps to keep the stock from drifting too close to the High Rim; the Association maintained line camps on the Flats for the housing of their summer crews.

Only the knowledge that Jord Ramont and his timber cutters were still infesting the lower foothills kept Buck Temple from volunteering to spend this summer above the High Rim as a member of Waterby's crew.

With Broken Bit nearly logged off, the question remained to be solved as to whether Ramont would succeed in hanging onto his railroad contract. If he did—a feat Temple had written off as impossible, owing to the slowness and inefficiency of wagon transport—Ramont's next move might be to invade the government timber between the High Rim and Arrowhead Creek canyon. On that eventuality depended the future existence of the cattle business in these foothills. If Ramont succeeded in tapping their watershed coverage, expanding into a wholesale logging industry which might continue for years to come, then Temple's one-man campaign would have been for naught.

The last night of the spring calf gather and trail drive to higher graze found every ranch in the Association represented by its boss or its foreman at the Goose Creek line camp.

The cattle, exhausted by their two-day drive up the steep slopes through the break in the High Rim, were bedded down on the near flats like a herd on a thousand-mile cross-country drive. The animals would not be bunched in such a concentration as this again until the beef gather in September.

Because the sheer, thousand-foot dropoff of the High Rim was so near at hand, waddies drew straws for the night shifts of herd duty, knowing that a coyote's howl or even such a small thing as a shooting star could touch off a stampede which, if it should head toward the Rim, could result in the loss of hundreds of prime cattle.

Buck Temple found himself paired with old Si Larbuck for the first shift. At midnight they were relieved by two Diamond X night hawks assigned to their sector of the bed-ground and, both men, feeling the accumulated fatigue of these past weeks of grueling labor in saddle, returned to the line camp soddy, and climbed into their bunks.

It was the sound of far-off gunnery and distant shouts of panic-stricken night herders that roused Buck Temple in the black hour between the false and the true dawn.

Not bothering to haul on his boots, Temple rushed to the door of the soddy in time to catch the first ominous rumble of thousands of cloven hoofs beating the sod out yonder toward the High Rim dropoff.

His yell of "Stampede!" brought his fellow waddies tumbling from their bunks. Dimly in the starlight, they saw the herd milling toward the yawning infinity of those ragged cliff brinks; they saw the flash of guns as fast-charging riders assaulted the flanks of the herd.

Over in the cavy corral the remuda horses were snorting in panic, frenzied by the contagious terror of a stampede in the making.

A lone rider hammered across the grassy flats to fling himself from saddle in front of the cabin. It was old Tex Waterby, boss of the Diamond X; the old stockman's left arm dangled at his side and his dusty sleeve was blood-soaked.

"Raiders jumped the herd from the Goose Creek break," Waterby choked out, falling from saddle into Temple's arms. "I seen Joe Redwine bein' stirrup drug to hell after a bushwhacker's slug hit him where the suspenders cross. Our beef's bein' shoved over the Rim, boys."

Chapter 14

Approaching dawn lit the eastern skyline like a pool of clotting blood. Against that red light the half-dressed cowboys massed in front of the line camp soddy could see the silhouetted blot of the stampeding herd being hazed ruthlessly toward the sheer brink of the High Rim to certain destruction.

Waterby had fainted; two Diamond X waddies took over their wounded boss, allowing Buck Temple to join the rush of angry men who jammed the soddy, hauling on boots and shirts, snatching up gunbelts and booted Winchesters.

"Ramont's bunch is back o' this," somebody said loudly in the confusion. "Figgers to throw the fear o' God into us and pave the way for makin' his timber deals with the weak-bellies in our string."

Temple, out at the corral throwing a saddle on his blue roan, knew that anonymous cowpuncher had hit the nail on the head. This was Ramont's retaliation for the blockade he had thrown across Arrowhead Creek. Temple found himself cursing his own stupidity for not having anticipated this blow the lumber faction was using to intimidate the foothill ranchers; now that it was upon him, the timing and this method of revenge seemed glaringly inevitable.

Temple was the first to ride away from the cavy corral. He was checking the magazine of his Winchester as he sent Blue rocketing across the Flats through brisket-high grass.

Behind him the Association reps were fanned out along a broad front, eyes squinting against dawn's golden glare as they sought out the fast-moving shapes of the raiders, now moving away in retreat from the scene of their outrage.

Gunfire crackled sporadically above the earth-shaking thunder of hoofs. Temple heard the whine of crisscrossing lead coming to meet the oncoming cattlemen.

There was no checking the advance of these men; having seen their beef plunging over the jagged line of the rimrock out yonder, they had been infuriated to reckless abandon which no leaden fusillade could halt.

Dust lifting from the hoof-trampled grass clouded the rays of the sun poised over the far desert rim and obscured the air enough to prevent identification of the stampede raiders who, their main objective accomplished in this surprise attack, were now streaking south toward the Goose Creek break which would let them down off the High Rim.

Temple, laying his shots toward those half-seen riders, knew one thing for certain—those renegades were not cowmen. They rode with an awkward, elbow-flopping stance, clumsily postured in saddle in the manner of men to whom fast-moving horses were an unfamiliar mode of transport.

There could be but little doubt that this catastrophe had been engineered by Jord Ramont; if not by his logging crew, then by gunhands imported to wreak Ramont's vengeance against the cattlemen who stood between him and his future expansion in this foothill timber.

Veering south to cut off the lead of the escaping raiders, Temple's horse shied violently away from some gruesome object in the trampled grass—a dead man.

That would be Joe Redwine of Rocking R, one of the night herders, first victim of the raiders' ambuscade. The attack had come too quickly for Redwine or Waterby or any of the other night patrol riders to shout a warning. Ramont, choosing his moment to strike when the Association's eggs were all in one basket, had achieved devastating surprise at the hour when sleeping men's vitality was drained to its lowest ebb.

By the time Buck Temple's roan had carried him to the mouth of the Goose Creek defile leading to the hills below High Rim, all view of the raiders was lost inside the throat of the creek's gorge.

Once off the Flats, Ramont's renegades could scatter like quail in the forest below, impossible to flush out. The fugitive riders would have every advantage; their guns could cut down every horse and rider who might attempt to follow them down the channel of that narrow, rock-ribbed side canyon.

Temple pulled his roan to a halt, reining around to wave the oncoming punchers back; this was no time to push the chase below the Rim into the full fire of hidden guns.

Taut-lipped, ashen-faced, the Association riders pulled up in a group around Buck Temple. From this point they had an unobstructed view of the ragged curvature of High Rim, stretching north-ward toward the far break of Stevens Pass.

Of the herd they had yesterday hazed up to the Flats for the summer, a scant third remained. Even as they watched, helpless to intervene, Temple and his saddle mates saw a jag of fifty or more animals suddenly spook and rush blindly over that sheer rim, to drop like a white-flecked, russet-brown waterfall into the awesome chasm below.

Down there a thousand dizzy feet from the cliff's edge, the talus lay in indigo shadow, not yet touched by the sun's dazzling brilliance; but the piled-up carcasses of mangled steers and fresh-branded yearlings could be seen mottling the steep tilt of crumbled boulders like spilled grain.

No living thing could survive that drop through empty space. Buzzards and coyotes would feast on that carrion for weeks to come. The clean, winelike air of this high country would reek with the stench of rotting beef until the furred and feathered scavengers had completed their work of stripping that pile of bones clean.

"Ain't we goin' after them bastards?" spoke up Hal Dikus. "What are we, a bunch of gutless cowards to stand here watchin' this thing while them bastards hightail it?"

Heads turned toward Buck Temple, tacitly acknowledging his leadership here in this group which numbered five ranch owners and as many foremen.

"Too late for that, Hal. We'd get picked off leaving the Rim. We've got to shove back what critters are left away from this wall."

The Lazy D boss leveled a shaking finger at Temple.

"This is yore fault, Temple. You and your blockin' that creek to Jord Ramont's logs. You might 'a' knowed you'd draw his lightnin'."

Grizzled old Si Larbuck spurred in fast to grab the gun out of Dikus' holster, reading the murderous light festering in the Lazy D man's eyes.

"I'll be damned if I'll listen to you cuss out the one man who had the guts to spike Ramont's guns this spring. Dikus!" Larbuck replied. "Not a doublecrossin' louse like you, who'd have sold out his timber to Ramont if Temple hadn't slowed him down. Cool off, now, damn it."

The cooler heads among the ranch hands, recognizing the wisdom of Temple's stand, began to break away from the group, forming a phalanx to work their way northward up the Skyline Flats. A morning's work remained here, putting crippled stock out of their misery, and searching for possible human victims of the brief, cataclysmic stampede.

Hal Dikus waited until Larbuck had emptied his Colt cylinder of shells and passed it back. Then the Lazy D boss turned his blazing eyes on Temple.

"I lost what beef I had this mornin'," Dikus panted. "All I got left now is what money Ramont will pay me for loggin' off the timber on my range. And, by God, I aim to let Ramont move in, soon as he's finished loggin' Broken Bit."

Larbuck fumed a profane epithet. "And let Ramont use Goose Creek canyon as a made to order road for loggin' off the government land above you and above the rest of us? Turn our range back to desert five years from now?"

Dikus yanked his reins savagely, spurring away.

"To hell with that," he yelled back. "I'm gettin' too old for cow-wranglin' anyhow."

Larbuck turned anguished eyes on Buck Temple.

"I got a good notion," the S Bar L man ground

out, "to put a slug in Hal Dikus' craw. This ruins us, son."

Temple's eyes held their bleak despair as he watched a group of riders loading Joe Redwine's corpse on a barebacked pony. He had no way of knowing how many other night herders had been victims of this stampede.

"Si," Buck Temple said heavily, "we've got a trackin' job to do this morning. We got to lay definite proof against Ramont in the sheriff's lap."

Larbuck cuffed back his battered hat and mopped his bald pate. "Yeah," the oldster growled. "We can't sic the law on Ramont for this job without definite proof his men done it. That oughtn't to be hard to do."

Hutch Inchcliff, foreman of Joe Redwine's Rocking R outfit, cantered up in time to hear Larbuck's last words,

"The boys are in favor of jumping Ramont's camp this mornin' and wipin' out them loggers to the last man," Inchcliff reported. "I don't think we can hold 'em back. I ain't so sure I'm in favor of holdin' 'em back. I'm the one who's got to let Missus Redwine know Ramont has made her a widow."

Buck Temple had his bad moment watching the cowpunchers gathering out at the line camp in the distance. They had the look of a lynch mob readying for a fight; all the signs were

193

there in these men spoiling for vengeance.

"We've got to handle this thing in a legal manner or we're lost, Hutch," Buck Temple said. "Larbuck and I are going to track down that bunch this morning. There ain't much doubt those raiders came from Broken Bit. But we've got to prove it. And when we ride on Broken Bit, the sheriff has got to be with us—or his deputy."

The Rocking R ramrod thought this over, common sense gradually cooling his rage.

"That way, we'd be a law posse instead of a lynch mob," Si Larbuck pointed out. "For Joe's sake, Hutch, try and keep those men from doin' anything rash before we got the deadwood on Ramont."

Inchcliff scowled uncertainly. "Those jaspers smell fresh meat and they're rarin' to go," he said. "I ain't sure I can keep 'em hobbled for long. They got to have some action to sink their teeth into."

Temple said quickly, "I realize that, Hutch. Tell you what. You assemble the men at some midway ranch—say Mort Overmile's Box O—and wait for Si and me to bring Mose Hartley back from town. Mose can swear us all in, if this deal involves raiding Jord Ramont's camp in force."

Inchcliff swung his horse around.

"Box O it is," he said. "We'll be waitin'. Us and every other cowpoke we can rustle up durin' the day."

Larbuck and Temple reined into Goose Canyon, picking up the easily read trail of the stampede raiders where they had stormed down the wide gulch in getaway.

Reaching the foot of the High Rim, they followed that trail below timberline without drawing a shot from any rearguard party the renegades might have left behind.

An hour later, in the heart of the timber, they found the clearing where the raiding party had rendezvoused, probably at sundown yesterday. From here, the trail became confused, hard to follow in the overall carpet of conifer needles.

They lost it completely at Goose Creek, but knowing the raiders must have kept to the water to destroy their sign, Larbuck and Temple separated to skirt each bank of the Goose, alert to pick up any evidence of a mounted party having left the creek bed.

It was grueling work, bucking the thick undergrowth down this long slope; the perpetual twilight thrown by the towering hemlock and ponderosa pines made spoor-hunting well-nigh impossible.

By midafternoon they had reached the canyon where the Goose boiled down into the broader canyon of the Arrowhead, joining that river a half mile north of Hal Dikus' Lazy D headquarters.

It was at this juncture of the streams that Si Larbuck and Buck Temple read the plain story of

Jord Ramont's hand in the grim tragedy enacted before dawn up on Skyline Flats.

The inbound hoofprints of the cattle stampeders were plain on the mud at the far side of the Arrowhead ford; this trail pointed straight north toward Broken Bit.

The evidence was conclusive, indisputable. The stampede raiders had returned to Ramont's camp.

Even as the two scouts sized up this damning evidence leading up the wagon road, two riders swung in sight from the direction of Broken Bit. Larbuck and Temple at once dropped hands to gunstocks; then they recognized the oncoming pair as Avis Malloy and her father.

The two cattlemen waited in grim silence as Genesee Malloy and the girl approached. Temple had not seen his fiancée since their meeting in the Trail House dining room on the eve of Temple's blockading of Arrowhead Creek. Throughout the calf round-up, Avis and her father had been living on Broken Bit, outside the orbit of Temple's riding.

Neither spoke as they came abreast of Buck and old Larbuck. Addressing Avis, Temple asked in a curt monotone, "Is Ramont back from his little jaunt?"

Avis and old Genesee exchanged glances which told them nothing. Then old Genesee spoke irritably. "What are you talking about? If you're here to stir up trouble, Buck, let me remind you this is Broken Bit ground, and that I own Broken Bit. Neither of you bronc stompers are welcome this far up the canyon."

Temple spurred his blue roan forward to prevent Malloy's attempted passing.

"You knew Ramont's boys were out horsebacking last night?"

Genesee made no answer. Avis caught Temple's eye and said coolly, "No loggers left the bunkhouse last night, Buck. I ought to know. I cooked breakfast for them this morning."

Temple's shoulders slumped. He pulled Blue around, signaling for Larbuck to let the riders by.

"Buck," Avis said suddenly, "we've got to have a talk. There's a lot that needs straightening out between us. We're on our way to town for supplies. If you'll join us—" Temple shook his head, anger needling him. He was thinking. A month ago, a week ago I'd have pawned my soul to enjoy an hour on the trail with you, Avis. Now I don't give a damn.

Aloud, he put his refusal in a cheerless drawl, "I guess not, Avis. Come on, Si."

He spurred off as if to return to the mouth of Goose Creek Canyon. After the Malloys had disappeared around a turn of the Rimrock wagon road, Larbuck overtook him and said gruffly:

"You made me swear never to mention Avis again, Buck. But you know she was lyin' about

Ramont's crew not leavin' Broken Bit last night, don't you?"

Temple's answer came in an anguished whisper, the gauge of his deep disillusion. "Yes, Avis lied. She's thrown in with Ramont. I'd be a fool not to admit it. It's a hard thing, Si, losing your trust in the woman you love."

Chapter 15

Larbuck turned away, embarrassed at this sight of a strong man's soul momentarily stripped naked. The old man knew what their next move must be; they had to reach Rimrock without delay and acquaint Sheriff Brockway with the evidence they had against Ramont's riders and this morning's tragedy below the High Rim.

Temple dragged a sleeve across his eyes. Hunger's acids were boring at his vitals; the ride down from the Skyline Flats had made his gunshot wound known with its steady throbbings.

"Si, you cut back along the west rim to where you can scout Broken Bit. It'll help later if you can testify in court that half of Ramont's logging crew was resting up in the bunkhouse."

Larbuck nodded, glad for this excuse to leave Temple alone with his thoughts. "You're headin' to town to fetch back a deputy?"

"Yeah. Mose Hartley, most likely. I'll pick you up on the way over to Mort Overmile's. We'll have our showdown with Ramont tomorrow mornin'."

After Temple had ridden off, following the wagon road down Arrowhead Creek Canyon toward Rimrock, Larbuck put his jaded horse back into the coulee of Goose Creek and thus gained the west rim of the Broken Bit range.

A mile north along that line of cliffs he came in sight of the logged-off expanse that had been Broken Bit, and the buildings making up Temple's outfit, mirrored in the pent-up artificial lake above Ramont's dam.

This scene filled the old S Bar L boss with a withering anger, realizing that the impending showdown with Ramont had come too late to benefit the one man who had brought it about. Broken Bit was ruined for all time to come, so far as summer grazing of cattle was concerned; a few years of spring thaws would strip the top soil of the ranch down to its bedrock bones.

Ramont's raid above the High Rim, intended to deteriorate the cattlemen's bargaining position, had in effect boomeranged against the lumber faction; the riders who even now were making a rendezvous at Overmile's Box O had been united by their common threat of bankruptcy. In the end, their might would drive Jord Ramont out of these hills. The moment Buck Temple got back from the county seat with a law officer, showing him the irrefutable proof of Ramont's part in the Skyline Flats outrage, would mark the beginning of the end of the logging threat to this country.

Larbuck picketed his gelding behind a tamarack grove out of sight of the Broken Bit ranch house and made his way to the rimrock, squatting on his haunches and putting his full attention on Ramont's camp.

Below the dam, Ramont's sawmill carriage was rumbling ceaselessly, powered by a donkey engine, as the four-foot saw took its slices through trundling logs. A train of tandem-hitched Conestoga wagons were loading heavy dimension lumber at the mill's loading ramp, preparatory for heading down Arrowhead Creek Canyon toward the Pass.

The sun was westering into the lithic teeth of the Cascade divide, but Larbuck's ears detected no interruption in the ring of axes and the occasional splintering crashes of falling trees up in Glacier Canyon. He took this as proof that Ramont was working his men around the clock in order to keep up production to meet his Pacific & Western contract.

A caravan of empty wagons, drab with the soda and alkali of the Columbia Basin desert, rounded the Rimrock road into Larbuck's view and drew up alongside the tie mill. Here, before the old cowman's eyes, Broken Bit was bleeding to death, killing Buck Temple's personal future.

As night spread its layers of indigo shadow over Broken Bit, Si Larbuck saw Jord Ramont leave the ranch house, carrying a lantern, and make his way out to the long tent which served his crew as a bunkhouse.

"The raiders who shoved our beef over the

Rim are sleepin' in there right now," ground the words across Larbuck's teeth. "I got to go down there and size 'em up at close range. We got to know definite what targets we'll be gunnin' for tomorrow, when Buck gets back with Hartley."

Invading Broken Bit lonehanded would be a desperately risky business, even under cover of darkness; but the memory of that wanton slaughter below the High Rim this morning was something that had more or less unhinged Larbuck, making him wholly reckless and irrational where his own safety was concerned.

Having made his decision, Larbuck set about putting it into action. With only the stars to guide him, Larbuck led his gelding down a side draw directly opposite the Broken Bit ranch house, on the far side of the log-floating holding pond.

Ramont's bunkhouse tent had been pitched at the very edge of a stand of pines across the canyon. The old S Bar L boss was obsessed with a determination to reach that tent and imprint on his memory a count of the faces of the riders Ramont had sent against the Association's pool herd last night. If he waited until those men were mingling at supper with the loggers from upper Glacier Canyon, segregating them would be impossible.

Larbuck was skirting the artificial lake's west shoreline, intending to cross to the far side by way of the dam itself, when a gunshot blasted echoes off the cliffs behind him and a slug sprayed gravel over his gelding's brisket.

He was discovered. Knowing he might have to shoot his way out of this trap, Larbuck jerked his six gun and pulled up, searching the clotting roundabout darkness for the source of that shot. His nostrils were keening the night for drifting gunsmoke when Jord Ramont's yell broke the brooding darkness.

"It's old man Larbuck, spying us out. Block him off this side of the mill road."

Ramont's voice came from somewhere across the dammed-up creek. Off to the south, responding to their boss' order, Si Larbuck heard the wagoneers and sawmill workmen yelling to each other as they deployed into position to block his retreat.

Larbuck realized too late that he had been spotted before sundown, up there on the rim; that all this while Ramont had been laying his trap, by now might have men circled behind him.

Larbuck wheeled his gelding and dug in the guthooks, putting his mount at a hard run toward the Rimrock road down canyon.

Gun flashes broke the night from the row of empty freight wagons lined up at the tie mill; all lanterns there had been extinguished, and the donkey engine had been shut down.

Fifty yards short of the dam, Larbuck felt his gelding break stride as a fresh burst of firing broke out; and he knew a stray slug had nicked his horse.

Larbuck held his own fire, riding Indian fashion on the pony's withers, as he heard the fast beat of running hoofs coming down the lakeside behind him.

A shotgun blasted deafeningly from the wagon road dead ahead of Larbuck as the dam wheeled past his left hand. The flash of the twin bore flames gave Si Larbuck a pinched-off glimpse of big Bull Corson, the high-climber, who had run out from the mill to head him.

The swarming buckshot plowed into the gelding's forelegs; as the running animal went down, Larbuck kicked his boots clear of stirrups and landed sprawling between the ruts, not twenty paces from where Ramont's big high-climber was slipping fresh shells into his sawed-off greener.

Lying there with his chin rammed in the dirt, momentarily dazed, Larbuck had a view of Bull Corson's gargantuan shape limned against the V notch of Arrowhead Creek Canyon.

Corson was coming toward him at a shuffle, shotgun held low, ready to pulverize his target with a point-blank hail of shot. Without conscious volition, knowing only that he had to kill or be killed, Larbuck lifted his arm out of the dust and caught the high-climber between his .45 sights.

Larbuck pulled trigger by pure reflex, the big gun bucking in hard recoil against the crotch of his hand. He saw Corson's advance halted by the slamming impact of the slug; the high-climber's fingers jerked the twin triggers of the scatter-gun, to blast a dusty eruption from the dirt at his own feet.

Behind Larbuck was the real danger; doom was racing down with that pandemonium of hoofbeats and yells and so far aimless shooting. It seemed an eternity before Corson's big legs gave way and pitched the dead logger to the ground.

The old S Bar L boss climbed to his feet, knowing there was no time left now to retrieve the Winchester from the saddle boot under his slaughtered gelding.

A stiff wind was sweeping up the canyon in his face as he started slogging down the road, punching fresh shells into his smoking Colt.

Corson's shooting had demoralized the cordon of wagon drivers, who had no real stake in this issue; Larbuck got through that thin line of gunmen without drawing their fire.

He heard Jord Ramont's following riders rein up as they reached the corpse of their high-climber sprawled in the dirt at the fork of the mill's side road. Having killed a Ramont man, Larbuck was under no illusions as to his chances for mercy if he were run down.

A horse's whicker came from the darkness ahead; Larbuck remembered having seen several head of saddle stock grazing without guards, down here where the forest pinched in toward the road.

Larbuck left the road, bucking knee-deep grass until he stumbled over a picket rope. Ramont's riders were spreading out behind him now, forming a line from cliff to cliff; the lumbermen, knowing Larbuck was afoot somewhere ahead of them, were intent on beating the brush of the canyon until they had flushed him out.

Jerking the picket pin out of the turf, the old ranchman followed the rope to the unsaddled mustang it held. He felt the gummy wetness of the animal as he mounted, and knew this mustang had been on the High Rim raid last night, turned out to graze without benefit of a rubdown. Trust these logging sons not to know or care enough to curry a gaunted horse.

Hitting the road at full gallop, Larbuck knew Ramont's pursuers had caught his scent when a fresh volley of gunfire blasted along a wide arc behind him and he heard the rattle of lead questing the trees on either side.

The mustang was not capable of sustaining a gallop over a long period. By the time Larbuck reached the fork where Goose Creek met the Arrowhead, he knew that Ramont had cut down his lead by half.

Hammering past the spot where he and Buck had met the two Malloys this afternoon, Larbuck groaned with despair as, hipping around, he saw white dust boiling up against the blackness of the timber as Ramont and his killer-crew broke out of the timber not a hundred yards behind.

The loggers spotted Larbuck at the same instant; flames spat from a dozen rifles at once, and at this range such a fusillade of converging lead could not miss.

Larbuck did not feel the random bullet which knocked him off the faltering mustang. He was skidding his beard through the roadside weeds when he heard the mustang go down, bullet-riddled.

Larbuck tried to rise, and only then did he discover that his left leg was useless, the bone shattered above the knee joint by the bullet that had unhorsed him.

It was the high wind roaring up the canyon that gave Si Larbuck his desperate idea for self-preservation. Nothing short of a wall of blazing timber could hold back Ramont's riders now. Already he could hear the lumber boss rallying his men for the final close-in fight.

Dragging his bleeding leg, Larbuck clawed his way into the deep underbrush. His hands shook uncontrollably as he fished a waterproof matchbox out of his Levi's. When he had a flame going he ignited a dead hemlock scrub, saw it burst aflame from roots to crown like an oil-soaked Christmas tree.

Larbuck fell back into cushioning licorice ferns, knowing the sudden glare of red firelight made him a sure target. Within seconds, it seemed, the gale had showered its spray of blazing hemlock needles into the further conifers.

A hundred-foot pine went up in flame instantly; the wind caught the blaze and lifted it across the further trees.

As Larbuck burrowed deeper into the brush down canyon, he saw the fire he had set jump the road as wind-borne sparks pelted the opposite underbrush. Like flame following a fuse, the forest fire licked at unbelievable speed along both walls of Arrowhead Creek Canyon, the wind carrying the heavy smoke in a billowing pall over the dismayed loggers massed in front of the Goose Creek ford.

Ramont's crew would know the full gravity of the holocaust which was sweeping down on them as fast as a galloping horse. With the wind blowing at such a velocity, Ramont would know that Larbuck's desperate counter move could bring a conflagration which in a few hours' time could gut Broken Bit, invade Glacier Canyon and lay waste to untold hundreds of square miles of pine and fir.

Larbuck saw Ramont's horsemen turn and head back up the road out of sight, the pillowing masses of smoke erasing his view of Goose Creek's mouth. The old rancher felt no elation, not even relief at having saved his own life.

Here in the Cascade country, setting the forest ablaze was a crime which was so monstrous it had no adequate punishment short of the lynch rope. Seeing the red wall of leaping fire writhing heavenward before the thrust of the gale, Si Larbuck felt an awesome sense of guilt course though him. Objectively speaking, his life was not worth the damage he had caused.

The wind kept the oppressive, withering heat away from Larbuck. But the bullet wound in his leg was sapping his vitality, and he knew he was fast weakening from loss of blood.

He was ripping his shirt off his back to make a compress to stem the flow of blood under his bullet-punctured overalls when two riders nearly rode him down, coming from the south.

Larbuck recoiled, gun lifting, believing that somehow Jord Ramont had sent a couple of riders ahead of him, cutting him off.

Then he recognized Buck Temple and Mose Hartley, the latter's star gleaming red in the reflected glare of the holocaust which was gutting Broken Bit.

The old man had to yell to make himself heard above the lash of the gale and the muffled organ roar of the forest fire. He was vaguely aware of the deputy sheriff reaming the neck of a whisky bottle between his lips; the liquor was an anesthetic, sparing Larbuck the agony which

Buck Temple's examination of his leg wound caused him.

There was no possibility of reaching Goose Creek Canyon now, thus getting out of the Arrowhead's gorge and riding on to keep their rendezvous with the cowmen who would be waiting for them at Overmile's ranch.

Larbuck's senses mercifully blanked out while Temple was loading him aboard his own blue roan. They were roping the wounded man to horn and stirrups when a sudden darkening of the flame-reddened night warned Temple and the deputy of a new peril rushing down to meet them from the direction of Broken Bit.

Above the howl of the night wind came the deafening roar of live steam hissing through the canyon; blending with that noise was the deeper crescendo of fast-moving waters plunging down canyon, snapping trees like matchsticks.

"Ramont's dynamited his dam, Mose!" Temple shouted to the deputy, at the same time vaulting Blue's rump and spurring out to the road. "He's flooding the canyon to save his mill and wagons and the ranch buildings."

It was a scene beyond human comprehension, this swift sprawl of unleashed tidal wave which bore down through the burning timber, quenching every spark that lay in its path.

Hemmed in by a high rock wall and the deep bed of the Arrowhead, there was no place for

Temple and the deputy to turn for safety, no hope of out-racing that oncoming wall of water which, before their dismayed eyes, was blotting out Larbuck's forest fire as quickly as it had advanced.

Jord Ramont had shown rare quick thinking in doing the only possible thing to save Broken Bit and the lives of his own crew—loosing the pent-up waters of his holding pond, letting the elements make a death struggle of it.

Temple and Hartley saw the white face of the flood's crest bearing down on them, and turned their horses to meet its impact. The impounded flood was too great for the shallow Arrowhead creek bed to contain, as Ramont had known.

But there was not enough volume of water to doom the riders in its path. Temple knew that, when he saw how the advancing flood was shallowing out, geysering spouts of spray lifting each time the flood hit a boulder or a charred stump. Every such obstacle lessened the force of the water that would be hitting them in the next few seconds.

Their horses snorted in panic as the frothing wave surged down the road, brimming the creek bed beside them. Spray engulfed horses and riders, but the waters were only hock deep, its force rapidly slackening off as the flood spent itself down the canyon behind them.

The Cascade foothills had, in the space of a few

dramatic minutes, been spared the devastating consequences of a wind-driven fire. But as the gurgling and draining noises of angry water subsided and Buck Temple was swinging his roan around toward Rimrock and medical help for the unconscious man in his saddle, he told the deputy sheriff glumly:

"Ramont did more than save Broken Bit from being burned out tonight, Mose. This flood has wiped out those outlaw tracks I brought you up to Goose Creek to look over. That leaves us without a bit of proof that Ramont's loggers were behind that beef stampede up on the High Rim."

Chapter 16

Rimrock's courthouse clock was chiming three o'clock when Mary Wunderling cantered out of the early morning fog astride her pinto. The cow town was asleep, its saloons and gambling dives locked up for lack of trade; the only light showing was in Doc Kildenning's shanty on a side street.

This was the homestead girl's first visit up the Pass since the night of Temple's showdown with Jord Ramont in the Timberline. She was here now in answer to an urgent summons which old Captain Collie had flashed in Morse code by means of a gas lantern.

That old derelict was waiting at the Arrowhead Creek bridge when the girl rode in. He was shivering with exposure, although he had draped himself in a greasy poncho made from a Hudson's Bay blanket.

"Buck Temple's waitin' over at Doc's with Si Larbuck, Mary," Captain Collie explained. "When he ast me to signal you, he didn't intend you should ride up here tonight."

She said, "It's all right, Cap. Si's my nearest neighbor. He's been a good friend. If he needs me, he needs me right away."

Buck Temple stepped out of Kildenning's as

Mary dismounted in front of the doctor's home. She was shocked by the deep-lined fatigue which the spring round-up and the ordeal of the past thirty-six hours had graven on his face. Temple looked as gaunt as she remembered him that day when she had fished him out of a blood-spattered snowbank below Grapevine Curve.

"I only asked Collie to find out if I could bring Si Larbuck down to your place tomorrow, Mary," Buck apologized. "If that old gaffer told you I wanted you up here tonight—"

"I couldn't sleep, Buck. How is Si? What happened?"

He told her of Larbuck's mantrap at Broken Bit, touched briefly on the forest fire and Ramont's countering flood, the waters of which filled Rimrock with a dull thundering even now.

"Larbuck will need nursing care for a couple of months, if he's ever to walk again," Buck finished up. "Doc has no hospital facilities here. Aunt Molly's still got her hands full taking care of Canuck. I thought—"

She took his arm, heading him up the path toward the house.

"Of course, Buck. Si's welcome at my place always."

They found the old rancher still under chloroform on the table where Doc Kildenning had probed for the .45-70 bullet and set the shattered bone. Mary Wunderling heard groans issuing from Kildenning's other room; Tex Waterby and two other injured men had been brought down from Skyline Flats during the night.

"Collie let me know about the High Rim raid before sundown yesterday," Mary said, accompanying Buck outdoors to get away from the reek of chloroform. "What does that add up to, Buck?"

Temple made no attempt to minimize what Ramont's stampede had cost the foothill cattlemen.

"Bad enough to leave Ramont in a position to buy timber rights almost anywhere he chooses," he said. "We can't prove Ramont was back of that ride after his floodwaters erased the proof Larbuck and I discovered. It's our word against his—and against Avis and Genesee Malloy's."

Mary Wunderling shuddered despite the enveloping fleece collar of her horsehide coat.

"This Rimrock country has been a troublespot since before Dad came here to settle," she mused. "Where will it all end, I wonder? How many graves will be dug before the issue between cows and lumber is settled?"

With no destination in view, they were now approaching the intersection of Main Street.

"The cowmen are all set to move in on Broken Bit and drive Ramont forcibly out of the hills," Buck said. "They're massed over at Mort Overmile's place right now. The sheriff sent Mose

Hartley over to Box O to warn them against taking the law into their own hands. A showdown now would only antagonize the Territorial Government against our cause."

Mary said heavily, "Then Ramont is to go unpunished for what he did up on the Flats yesterday?"

Temple shrugged. "Who can point to any one of his loggers and say with truth, 'You helped raid our pool herd, therefore, you are under arrest'? I don't know the answer, Mary. I only know that the day is fast coming when Ramont and I will settle our own score with gunsmoke."

They were at the edge of Main Street now; besides the night lights in the Trail House lobby ahead of them, the only part of this town which was awake tonight was the Mountain Express stage station, where the post office had been transferred after the killing of Karl Gothe and the closure of his Mile-High Mercantile.

A saddle horse and pack mare were waiting in front of the stage office, proof that Jingo Paloo was in there making ready for another circuit of the outlying ranches on his mail route.

"Mary," Temple found himself saying as a new line of thought entered his head, "Paloo needs you as badly as you need him. Why don't you two get together on this before you waste your youth away? Don't you know Jingo can't sleep good nights for worrying about you living alone down there at the foot of Coppertooth?"

Their stroll was taking them past the long façade of the boarded-up Mile-High Mercantile now. Ahead of them a few yards was the spot where old Captain Collie had led Sheriff Brockway to view Karl Gothe's dead body. The memory of what had happened here put its edge on Mary's voice as she halted and looked up into Buck Temple's eyes.

"You think a lot of Jingo, don't you, Buck?"

He said, "Next to Canuck Brockway, he's the truest friend I have in these hills. We grew up together."

She reached out to touch his hands.

"What makes you think Jingo loves me?"

Temple took a long time about the business of shaping himself a smoke and lighting up. He was harking back in memory to the night of his release from Walla Walla Penitentiary, when Paloo had first told him how he felt about Mary Wunderling.

"Mary," he said finally, "there are things a man should properly say for himself. He loves you. He wants to marry you. He has told me so."

The girl's body touched his; she was standing that close, her eyes lustrous and thoughtful. At any moment Jingo Paloo would be stepping out of the stage office with his mailsacks, to see them here. It was Jingo Paloo who should be standing beside Mary Wunderling in such intimacy as this.

Her nearness brought a return of that over-powering hunger Temple had first felt for her lips during his brief stay under her roof; it filled him with a sense of disloyalty to Jingo Paloo and a burning disgust for himself.

"Buck," the girl whispered, "what makes you think Jingo is the man I love?"

Her words shocked him, their inference too clear to be mistaken; he recalled sharply the thinly veiled admission of defeat which Jingo Paloo had made the night he left his vigil over the Arrowhead Creek blockade—the night Paloo had said, *"Mary's got her heart set on another hombre. How blind can a man be, amigo?"*

But whatever Temple's answer might have been, Mary was not to know.

The doors of the Trail House swung open to spotlight them in a fanwise spread of light from the lobby; against that light Avis Malloy and her father were silhouetted as they walked out to where their saddle horses stood hitched and waiting at the rack, along with two pack mules buried under diamond-hitched loads of supplies for Broken Bit's lumber camp.

Old Genesee Malloy's gaze flashed across the street to recognize Buck Temple, and that recognition brought an oath from his lips. Leaving Avis beside the horses, Malloy stalked over to confront Temple at arm's length.

"Larbuck murdered Bull Corson last night," the

old man said. "The word has reached me about Larbuck trying to burn me out. That was why you and Si were snooping around the canyon yesterday afternoon, wasn't it?"

Temple felt all his built-up hatred for this man surfacing.

"Malloy, if you were twenty years younger, I'd knock you down. Burning out my ranch wouldn't hurt you—if hurting you was in my mind."

Old Genesee hooked thumbs in the cartridge belt strapped outside his mackinaw. He had never bothered to mask his hostility of Buck Temple in the past; his feelings were plain now.

"I aim to swear out a warrant for Si Larbuck's arrest on charges of first degree murder, Buck. I might sic the law on you as an accessory in Corson's murder."

Only the tempering presence of Mary Wunderling at his side kept Temple's rising anger in check now.

"Ramont won't let you push Larbuck into court. You'll find out why when you get back to Broken Bit this morning."

Malloy started to turn, only to have Temple seize his arm. "It wouldn't surprise me if you weren't riding with that bunch who raided our beef up on the High Rim yesterday, Genesee. If you were, this country ain't big enough to hold you. That's as much warning as you'll get from me."

Genesee broke Temple's grasp on his sleeve and stalked back to where Avis was waiting with the horses.

Mounting, Malloy picked up the trail ropes of his pack mules and called angrily across the street:

"You thought by gettin' Corson shot that you'd hamstring Ramont's loggin' operations, Buck. You can guess again. I was a high-climber myself before I bought out Trail House and came here to retire. I'm takin' Bull's place in the woods."

Getting no answer, Malloy raged on, "By noon today I'll be crowning the last spar tree we'll rig in Glacier Canyon. With my own hands I'll set the crown block so Ramont can high line the last of his timber off of your spread. When Broken Bit is cleaned out, we'll move to Hal Dikus' place. I'll live to see the last cow starved out of these hills, Temple."

Malloy roweled his big horse savagely, the dust of his down-street gallop drifting back to cover Buck Temple and Mary.

Avis Malloy had not followed; she put her horse across the street now, staring down at Mary Wunderling with a cold smile touching the corners of her mouth.

"I'd like to speak to my fiancé privately, Mary."

Mary Wunderling shrugged, gave Temple's hand a quick pressure and headed down-street toward the Mountain Express office, where Jingo Paloo at that moment was loading up his mail pony.

"There's nothing you and I have to talk over, Avis," Temple said wearily.

The girl smiled softly. "But there is, Buck. The most important thing in the world to us. Setting our wedding date."

The abruptness of her words, the last thing Temple had expected to hear from her at a time like this, held the cowman speechless.

"Dad was bluffing about starving out this country," Avis said gently. "Last night a purchasing agent for the Pacific & Western Railway reached Rimrock. He brought word that Jord's contract has been canceled. P & W will get its timber from the Okanogan, Buck. You have won your fight."

Anger came in to fill the vacuum in Buck Temple's being.

"So Ramont's on the downgrade, and you turn back to me, Avis? Figuring my prospects are the better of the two?"

Avis Malloy stiffened, stung by the bitterness of his words.

"Buck, it's never been anyone but you where I was concerned. Surely you know that. When Jord Ramont cleans up Glacier Canyon, he'll be moving his mill out of these hills forever. Can't you see that nothing stands between—"

Temple cut her off with an angry lift of his hand that was like a physical slap.

"If Ramont leaves Rimrock, you'd better go with him, Avis. You and I are finished."

He turned his back to her, heading toward Doc Kildenning's. Remembering something, he halted, ignoring Avis Malloy's stockstill posture in saddle, and called over to where Mary Wunderling stood in front of the stage stand with Jingo Paloo:

"I'll bring Si Larbuck down in a wagon, Mary. No need of you waiting in town."

The clangor of Rimrock's fire bell roused Buck Temple out of a troubled slumber at ten-thirty. He had made himself a bed in Kildenning's barn; until the bell roused him he had slept like a drugged man.

Only in times of direst emergency was the firehouse bell sounded like this. Temple reached Main Street in time to see crowds of men converging from the buildings to gather in front of the volunteer brigade firehouse.

A man he recognized as one of Jord Ramont's timber fallers was seated astride a lather-flecked horse, addressing the Rimrock populace as Buck Temple came up.

"The fire's spreadin' through that prime timber this side of Glacier Canyon. Must have caught from that burn we thought we'd flooded out last

222

night. If the wind shifts this way there's nothin' to keep it from wipin' out the whole town. Ramont sent me for help. That blaze has got to be put under control for the good of ever'body."

Old Captain Collie, half drunk even at this early morning hour, cackled sarcastically as the crowd's self-appointed spokesman. "So you want this town to save Ramont's bacon? To hell with you and your breed! Might as well let Nature take keer of strippin' the timber offen these hills as leave it for a bloodsucker like Ramont to do."

Collie's opinion was shared by the men; as Buck Temple elbowed his way through the crowd toward the logger's horse, he saw that Ramont's man was afraid for his own safety in the face of this suddenly hostile mob.

Temple climbed up on a fire hose cart and raised his arms to silence the Rimrock crowd.

"This has nothing to do with saving Ramont's bacon, men," Temple shouted. "A change in wind direction could bring the fire straight down Arrowhead and level this town before sunset."

The crowd shifted uneasily, eyes already watching the ugly roll of smoke clouds which were racking up in sinister shapes beyond the north wall of Coppertooth Pass.

"Hitch up wagons and load every barrel and bucket you can find," Temple ordered. "Every man who can rustle up a horse for himself hit the trail for Broken Bit. Bring along shovels and sacks, anything you can find to fight fire with. A few plows would help."

Ten minutes later, Buck Temple was heading his blue roan up the Arrowhead Creek road, in the lead of a fire-fighting force which numbered close to fifty men, most of them property owners in Rimrock.

He saw Mary Wunderling on her pinto, riding with this group; there was no time to argue against her coming on this mission.

When he reached the burned-out, flood-muddied area where Ramont's floodwaters had wiped out Si Larbuck's blaze last night, Temple could see the ugly wall of leaping flame on both sides of Glacier Canyon's walls.

Ramont had every available logger and mule whacker up there, combating the blaze. The wind still bore from the south, menacing the virgin timber beyond Glacier Canyon. But the wind was a fickle thing; the fire must be halted at any cost if these foothills were to be spared total destruction.

Temple headed on up the Arrowhead, coming in sight of the drained lake above Ramont's dam. It was his intention to ride on past his former ranch and launch his own fire-fighting efforts beyond the present limits of the blaze.

Instead, he found himself reining up at the Broken Bit ranch house, where Avis Malloy and

Jord Ramont were arguing about something by the front gate.

Seeing Temple, Avis broke away from the lumber boss and ran toward him, her face streaked with dirt and tears, her eyes white-sprung with the horror that gripped her.

"It's Dad, Buck!" screamed the girl, incoherent in her terror. "Jord won't lift a hand to save him."

Jord Ramont strode up behind the girl, the mutual hatred between these enemies shelved for the time being in the face of whatever personal disaster had come to Avis.

"Genesee topped Corson's spar tree at the end of Glacier this morning," Ramont explained. "He's not the high-climber he used to be, and the tree split on him when the crown fell. It pinched him between the tree and his safety belt. If Genesee isn't already dead, he's just as good as dead. I'll send no man into that canyon with the fire on both sides of it."

Avis Malloy was clinging to Temple, her eyes imploring him with a panicked desperation.

"Dad's hanging helpless two hundred and fifty feet up," she cried hoarsely. "He isn't dead, Buck. I just came from there. Jord won't send a climber to bring him down."

Temple glanced over at Jord Ramont, saw the lumber boss shrug.

"All my men are busy fighting that fire Larbuck set. I can't ask a man to risk being burned alive, trying to get a doomed man off that spar pole. The fire would be there before any man could reach Genesee."

Buck Temple reached down to lay a hand on Avis's shoulder.

"I'll do what I can," he said brusquely. "I'd do as much for a crippled dog. Ramont, loan me a pair of climbing hooks and some safety harness. I'll take my chances of out-racing that fire to where Genesee is."

Chapter 17

Rimrock's fire-fighting volunteers reached Broken Bit in time to see Buck Temple heading for Glacier Canyon at a reaching gallop, soon lost beyond the smudge of the smoke clouds funneling in off the rimrocks.

Lashed behind his cantle was a high-climber's safety gear and climbing spurs, furnished by Jord Ramont for this suicidal trek up a canyon already outflanked by the holocaust.

In Ramont's very readiness to provide Temple with the gear necessary to scale a spar tree, Temple had guessed the lumberman's ulterior purpose. He knew Ramont had written him off as lost; it would be a handy way of ridding himself of a foe whom he must otherwise meet in a showdown at gun's point.

As he put his blue roan into the looming maw of Glacier Canyon's side door to Broken Bit's range, Temple twisted in saddle to perceive another rider following. He felt a moment's pure alarm, recognizing Mary Wunderling and her pinto.

He reined up with the intention of turning her back; but a hundred-foot pine snag, blazing like a candle, crashed off the south rim with a heavy concussion, blocking the canyon's logging road.

That barrier would turn Mary back; in effect it sealed Buck Temple off, leaving him no other alternative than to continue on toward the canyon's blind end.

Reversing his neckpiece, Temple lifted it over his face to shield his cheeks from the pelting sparks. Giving Blue his head, he disappeared in the swimming void of a smoky tunnel, feeling the fire's hot pressure upon him from all sides.

Two miles up the logging road, he had out-raced the smoke and flame and was alone in the heart of Ramont's logged-off stumpland. The last remaining stand of marketable timber was ahead of him now; the tag-end of Ramont's logging operations on the Broken Bit, and if Avis's report of the canceled P & W contract was true, the end of Ramont's activities in Cascade County. It was to harvest this last pocket of timber that had brought Genesee Malloy far up canyon to rig a spar pole, work which Bull Corson would otherwise have done.

Rounding a turn of the canyon, Temple's horse nearly collided with a donkey engine mounted on a big sledge, which Ramont's crew had abandoned at the outbreak of the fire this morning. That donkey was to have provided the power to snake ten-ton logs out of the woods, utilizing cables attached to a crownblock on the top of the spar which Genesee Malloy had crowned off today.

It was unearthly dark here in the canyon; the sun was obscured by the ugly hood of smoke and the towering ponderosa pine growth on all sides.

His blue roan was nearing the end of its stamina when Buck Temple reached the logged-off clearing at canyon's end, in the center of which towered a lofty pine, denuded of its limbs and crown.

At the crest of this spar tree, high, very high above the ground, Buck Temple caught sight of Genesee Malloy's red shirt making its bright dot of color against the smoke-pearled gray of the sky.

The oldster looked like a grotesque bug, rather than any human shape; he was held to the splintered apex of the spar tree by his safety harness. A long-handled ax and a high-climber's saw dangled at ropes' ends below Malloy, swinging in the agitated air currents, flashing weirdly to remind Temple of old Captain Collie's heliograph.

At the tree's foot Temple flung himself from stirrups, and began the clumsy, unfamiliar job of buckling the high-climber's spurs to his boots. The life belt was a thick, unwieldy thing of laminated bullhide, studded with rivets. Its weight was such that, when he had finished buckling on the safety harness, Temple removed his holstered Colt and shell belt to lighten the burden he would have to lift to the pinnacle of this mighty tree.

High-climbing was a skilled art of the tall timber country; for a man of Temple's background, knowing little or nothing of a logger's techniques, it was a ten-minute job merely to swing the safety belt around the four foot bole of the pine and buckle it satisfactorily.

Sinking his hooks into the thick corrugations of the red bark, Temple began his ascent.

By the time he was thirty feet up, shifting the life belt ten times in that distance, Temple felt exhausted to the point where he was tempted to retreat.

But he forced himself to keep climbing, disregarding the slug of his overtaxed heart. He had no time to ask himself if saving Genesee Malloy's life was worth this risk to his own safety; it was something a man did without question.

He knew that the advancing forest fire could suck the oxygen out of the air and suffocate him long before the actual flames attacked this roundabout timber.

To Temple, this was an elementary thing, this attempting to whisk another human being out of a death-trap. Working his way to the blaze which Corson had marked "100 Ft.," Temple began to feel the heat of the down-canyon fire, now that he was nearing the level of the crown growth of surrounding trees.

As yet, he had seen no sign of life in Malloy's body up there. The oldster was either dead or insensible.

As the bole of the pine narrowed, climbing became easier. At the infrequent intervals when he had to anchor his spurs and take up the slack of his life belt, Temple rested. His shirt was sopping with his own sweat; his heart was like a hot mallet rapping his ribs in a tempo too rapid to count.

The deafening crackle of raw flames coming off the rim and dropping into the canyon timber spurred Temple to faster and faster effort. It dizzied him to look down the dwindling perspective of the tree under him.

Air currents, caused by the artificial draft drawn to the fire, were making the spar tree arc sickeningly. Temple wanted to vomit; he wanted to hang limp in his supporting belt and ease the intolerable strain on his muscles.

But he kept going, knowing time was fast running out for him as well as Malloy. The heat of the advancing fire was a furnacelike breath against his back, but his body was past registering pain now.

The first sparks stung his cheeks; fine ash was powdering the rough corrugations of the bark. Finally, exhaustion forcing him to rest, he looked up to discover that Malloy was alive.

The spar pole was fractured like a split matchstick for the last several feet of its length; that spreading Y of wood had squeezed Avis's father between the tree and his unyielding loop of safety harness. It was like being caught in the jaws of a giant vise; the pressure of it had squeezed the blood out of Malloy's ears and nose and mouth.

The old man's face was congested and black in the violence of his agony; but his limp-hanging arms twitched spasmodically, giving Temple his proof that this climb had not been leading him to a corpse.

Temple found himself thinking. This is the man who bought my ranch from Karl Gothe and sold out to Ramont. This is the man who has done everything in his power to keep Avis and me apart. This is a man who might have helped Ramont raid our beef up there on High Rim the other night.

He was a damned fool. But it was too late to worry about his reasons for being here.

Resuming his climb, Temple had to stop and fish in his chaps pocket for a stock knife, to cut the ropes which held the old man's topping ax and saw. Watching the tools plummet down, it seemed to Buck Temple that Glacier Canyon had turned into a solid flowing river of fire.

When Malloy's dangling boot toes brushed his shoulder, Temple inched his belt around to get it between the tree and the oldster's legs. He called out Malloy's name, but his voice was lost in the funneling roar of the advancing fire.

This high up, the air was clearer, but heated and fast losing its life-giving oxygen content. The spar pole's tip described wide arcs as the wind and heated air currents buffeted it; the swinging made the world below rock dizzily, nauseating Temple as no bucking horse had ever done.

He cut the ax and saw ropes from Malloy's belt and used these five-foot lengths of sturdy hemp to tie the old man's limp body securely to his own safety belt, knowing the thick leather would support them both during the descent to come.

Then, finding it impossible to unbuckle Malloy's gear, Temple used his knife to cut the old man free of the harness which had kept him from plunging to his death.

As Malloy's body dropped free, its weight jerked dangerously on the ropes tied to Temple's belt, threatened to dislodge his hooks from the shattered wood. Malloy's lips were moving, but whatever he said was lost in the roar of the fire seething up the canyon toward this clearing.

Temple thought, I haven't got a chance to make it back to the ground before the fire cuts me off completely. The two of us will roast up here like calves on a barbecue spit.

He began his descent by jerking his spurs out of the bark and letting the loop of the life belt slide a good ten feet vertically before checking their fall by flinging his weight back against the bight of the harness.

As the bole widened below the hundred foot blaze, this rapid mode of descent became increasingly difficult. He had to let out his safety belt every few yards to accommodate the increased girth of the tree; each time he did this brought a risk of having the belt's slack run through the buckle and drop them to their deaths.

Below ninety feet the air was thick with smoke. During a ghostly lull in the roundabout din, he heard Genesee Malloy's voice for the first time, the old man's blood-frothed lips close to his ear.

"Cut me loose an' save yourself, boy. I'm paralyzed. My back's broke. Cut me loose, Buck."

It was in that instant that the bullet struck the tree, perforating a slot in the taut life belt inches from Temple's face. At first, the cowpuncher believed that bullet hole in the bark was a figment of his overwrought imagination; then his ears caught the muffled whipcrack of a rifle shot above the roar of the burning forest.

"Somebody shootin' at us, Buck," Malloy shrieked in Temple's ear. "Figger it's the merciful thing to do before we fry."

Another bullet screamed like a hornet in the narrow space which separated Temple's head from Malloy's. He saw in the upward angle of the bullet's furrow through the pine bark that the gunman was somewhere at the edge of the canyon clearing.

Two more rifle shots sounded through the cacophony of the flames. Then a gust of wind cleared the surrounding smoke and Temple had a view of a horseman who sat his saddle fifty yards from the base of the spar tree.

Before Temple could identify that marksman, the smoke closed in again; but he knew the rider had a Winchester stock cuddled to his cheek, was drawing a deliberate bead on his helpless target eighty feet above the ground.

This was murder—not a mercy shooting. Someone had trailed him up Glacier Canyon, intent on killing both him and Genesee Malloy.

And then, off to the left and higher up, a sudden gunshot drew Temple's eye away from the ambusher's direction.

Limned against the black timber above the head of Glacier Canyon's box end, the buckskin-clad figure of Mary Wunderling was kneeling, her Springfield slanting across a granite boulder.

Temple thought wildly, Mary doubled back and circled the fire to get up here.

The girl was shooting as fast as she could load the army carbine. When Temple cranked his head around to stare at the ambusher's location, he was in time to see the rider spur his stallion out of sight in the boulder-strewn mouth of a side coulee which would be his mode of retreat from the crawling tidal wave of fire which had cut off the Broken Bit road.

Paradoxically, it became almost deathly quiet here, as Temple struggled painfully, yard by yard, down the tree. Mary Wunderling's gunfire had been silenced, her target now invisible in the side coulee.

Twenty feet above the ground, Buck came to a dead halt due to the constricting length of his life belt harness. He fumbled at the heavy bronze clasp of the buckle, the job of extending the belt made well-nigh impossible due to the awkward angle of Malloy's hanging body.

He felt the strap slipping through his numbed fingers, but all strength had left him and there was no stopping the belt now. It came free of the buckle with a slapping noise, and both men plummeted the remaining distance to the ground to hit the cushioning pile of boughs formed by the crown growth which Malloy had cut off.

That yielding foliage saved Buck Temple from a broken neck. He lay quiet for a moment, roped to Malloy, realizing that the old man had been knocked out by the impact of their fall.

He thought frantically, Can't wait here. Fire cut us off any minute.

He saw the white-red wall of the fire approaching through the trees down canyon. The exertion of trying to roll out from under Malloy's legs was too much; he felt his senses teeter, then skid over the rim of the black funnel that leads to oblivion.

Then all feeling was gone, all sensation; he was floating in a black void where fear and anger and fatigue had no pain at all, and no meaning for him.

Chapter 18

Mary Wunderling appraised her chances of reaching the spar tree and bringing Temple and Malloy out of the canyon's pit, and found the venture full of risk, promising almost certain death.

Knowing she could not force her pinto saddler to brave the hellish temperatures down there, she made her one concession to the possibility of not returning to the head of the canyon when she untied the pony's reins from a sapling and let the pinto bolt where it would.

Shouldering her canvas water bag, Mary Wunderling headed down the rocky declivity which formed Glacier Canyon's box end, head ducked before the extreme blistering heat.

When she reached the level of the clearing, one corner of her brain told her that the wind had shifted direction; it now quartered from the north, blowing the smoke and flame back upon itself.

If this was no passing, vagrant change in the wind, it would prove providential for the foothills and the whole future of this range. The wind had been accountable for the five-mile advance the conflagration had made in the last hour; if the wind continued to block the flames, the burn might be confined to its present area.

Sloshing water from the canvas canteen over her head, the girl pushed on through the wilted fernbrake and brush and approached the foot of the spar tree.

She had witnessed the final drop of the two men, from her vantage point on the canyon's brink; she had seen their bodies bounce and roll in the yielding crown growth and knew the fall had not been fatal; therefore, justifying her own approach into the danger area.

Temple's big blue roan was dancing nervously in the vicinity, loyalty for its fallen master countering the animal's instinct to bolt. Knowing it would be physically impossible for her to drag both men up the rocky end of the canyon, Mary veered over to snatch Blue's trailing reins and then, bracing herself against the hot breath of the flaming trees beyond the clearing, made her way to where the sprawled shapes of Buck Temple and the old man lay at the foot of the pine.

She felt for a pulse and found it in Temple's neck, and knew he was in no immediate danger of asphyxiation. She sloshed tepid water over the cowman's head and finished emptying her water bag over Genesee Malloy's bald scalp.

Neither man showed any sign of rallying out of his stupor. She found the knife in Temple's pocket and used it to cut both free of the ropes and safety harness.

Drawing on wellsprings of unguessed strength,

239

the girl hoisted Temple's inert bulk to a shoulder and half-carried, half-dragged him over to the roan.

Returning for Genesee Malloy, she knew from the grotesque twist of the oldster's torso that his spinal column had been snapped. From past experience the girl knew the extreme danger of moving a patient with a spine injury; but there was no time to rig up any kind of litter.

Compared to Temple, moving Genesee Malloy's skinny frame presented no difficulty. The blue roan shied as she struggled to hoist Malloy over the saddle; she tied him there with the rope still knotted around the old man's waist.

Buck's coil of pleated rawhide lass rope was buckled to the saddle pommel; Mary shook out a loop, got it under Temple's armpits and pulled him erect against the roan's shoulder. She took a half-hitch around his arms and drew them across the horse's withers, dallying the rope to saddle horn to support his hanging weight.

Then, picking up Blue's reins, the girl headed for the mouth of the side coulee through which Temple's ambusher had made his getaway.

She was vaguely surprised to find herself, some while later, on the grassy bench above the canyon, Malloy slumped slack across the saddle, Buck Temple still hanging bent-kneed against the pony's shoulder and foreleg.

She knew this was no time to halt, that safety

lay in getting above the potential path of the fire; but all power left her muscles and, utterly spent, Mary Wunderling fell face foremost on the grass in front of the double-laden horse.

Buck Temple was rubbing her temples with moist moss torn off a nearby windfall when she rallied out of it. His white-toothed grin was grotesquely accentuated by the heavy layers of soot and grime which veneered his flesh.

She gasped out something inarticulate, and heard Temple reassuring her. "Fire's doubling back on itself, Mary. We're safe here. And so is your pinto. He snagged his bridle on a branch."

Later, Mary was vaguely aware of Temple lifting her astride the pinto. She opened her eyes to see the cowpuncher mounting his blue roan, supporting Genesee Malloy in front of him.

She had no way of knowing how long she had been unconscious; but staring off across the bench into the smoke-fuming maw of Glacier Canyon, she saw ugly tongues of orange flame licking at the spar tree. The crown growth into which the two men had dropped was now a smoking mound of ashes.

Mary forced herself to speak. "Malloy can't take any pounding, Buck. His back is broken."

Temple nodded, his left arm shifting to ease the sagging weight of the old man.

"I know that. But we can't risk waiting here

in case the wind changes. If Broken Bit is still standing when we get back, I'll leave him with Avis and send a rider to town after Doc Kildenning."

They entered a game trail and shortly Buck Temple recognized the spot where timber cruiser Les McAllister's corpse had been found last November.

This was the ridge where the Rimrock trader, Karl Gothe, had been elk-hunting when he claimed to have seen Temple shoot McAllister from ambush. Passing this scene now, Temple mused that no man would ever know whether Gothe had seen logger Vance Bluedom earn his Judas pay when he shot the timber cruiser.

Riding steadily southward, following the shoulder of a ridge well above the burned-over area outside Glacier Canyon, Mary Wunderling recovered sufficiently to spur her pinto up alongside Temple's stirrup.

"We owe you our lives, Mary," she heard the big rider say. "This makes twice you've been at the right spot at the right time to save my bacon. Why did you follow me out of Broken Bit?"

"Because I saw Jord Ramont leave right after you did. I was afraid he might double around to wait for you at the spar tree at the end of the canyon."

Temple pulled up his horse suddenly, giving her his close and calculating attention.

"And did he? Was it Ramont taking those potshots at Malloy and me?"

Mary Wunderling gave him her direct stare.

"It was Ramont, Buck. Of course." Her glance dropped to the shiny spot on his chaps leg where his gun holster had hung. "We may run into him on this ride back. I think you had better take my gun."

She lifted a Remington six-shooter from the belt of her buckskin jacket and leaned out to hand it to him butt-first. He thrust it under the waistband of his Levi's.

"Thanks. Shucked my own gun harness at the foot of that tree. Mary, I don't think we'll see Ramont again. Avis tells me this railroad contract has blown up. He knows you spotted him trying to bushwhack us. That alone is enough to put him on the dodge."

They resumed their ride, scanning their trail with a strict caution, knowing that Jord Ramont had probably traveled this route ahead of them. The smoke hung thick as gauze along the ridge, bringing premature dusk to the day, but no longer was the ominous crackle of flaming brush and timber in their ears.

"Long as this north wind holds, the fire is licked," Temple said. "Broken Bit is gutted out, but no difference. It's not too much to pay if the rest of this range is spared."

Nearing the edge of the smouldering hillside

where the fire had broken over the west wall of Glacier Canyon, they saw a herd of staked saddle ponies bearing a variety of local ranch brands, and groups of riders busy down there with shovels and wet sacks, putting out pockets of fire and covering smouldering deadfalls.

"Cowboys," Mary Wunderling said wonderingly. "How could so many have reached here so soon?"

Temple knew the answer to that; the cattlemen who had assembled at Mort Overmile's ranch had seen the smoke and ridden here, their original purpose of invading Jord Ramont's camp put aside before this common danger and the fire's threat to their own destinies.

Coming in sight of the drained lake bed above the dam, Temple saw with overwhelming relief that Broken Bit had not been razed by the fire which had circled it.

He saw Deputy Sheriff Mose Hartley soaking a strip of burlap in a barrel which had been brought to the scene in a Rimrock wagon, and acknowledged the exhausted lawman's wave with an equally weary gesture.

They tipped down a side coulee and thus reached the Broken Bit ranch house. Avis Malloy came running out as she recognized her father's limp shape aboard Temple's roan.

As the girl came up, Mary Wunderling cried sharply, "Is Ramont here?"

The gaunt-faced girl shook her head, never taking her eyes off Genesee's slumped body.

"No. Jord's up the canyon with his crew cleaning up the fire on the east rim. Oh, Buck, how is he? Is he dead?"

Temple dismounted and carefully lowered Malloy from saddle.

"His back's broke, Avis. And bringing him down from the end of the canyon hasn't done him any good. But we couldn't risk leaving him up there in case the fire broke out again."

Mary waited with the horses at the front gate while Temple carried Malloy into his familiar ranch house, the house he and his father had built in a happier time, now gone forever.

Old Genesee was rallying back to consciousness when Temple lowered the gravely injured high-climber into a bed which Jord Ramont had requisitioned for his use.

"I'll go fetch the doctor," Temple said, suddenly aware of his own overpowering fatigue.

Avis was busy undressing her father. "No," the girl said. "I've already sent Jord's whistle-punk to town for Doc Kildenning. I—I was that sure you'd be back with Dad, Buck."

Avis crossed around the bed and flung her arms around Temple's neck, kissing him with a sudden wild abandon.

"You risked your life for Dad," Avis husked out, remorse goading her. "Knowing how hard he worked to come between us, Buck. But I—I'll spend the rest of my life making that up to you if you'll have me, Buck."

Doc Kildenning, his seamed face drenched with sweat from the strain of his hard ride out from Rimrock, bustled into the room at that moment, black satchel in hand. He went at once to Genesee Malloy's bedside, pursing his lips gravely as he checked his patient's respiration and pulse.

"I'll need hot water," the medico said. "Your father is as close to fraying out his string as he's likely to get, Avis. But I think we can save him."

Out in the kitchen, Temple drank copiously and pumped a dipper of water to take out to Mary Wunderling.

He found that Mary had tied their two horses at the front fence and had flung herself in a hammock in front of the house.

He was holding the dipper to her lips when Avis came to the front door and called brokenly, "Dad's awake and wants to see you, Buck. Can you come? And hurry?"

Temple reached down to touch Mary Wunderling's brow.

"Don't leave," he said. "As soon as I can, I want to get back to town and get Si Larbuck moved out to your homestead. I want to go back with you, Mary."

She said, "I'll be here, Buck," and closed her

eyes, the tension flowing out of her as she relaxed in the hammock.

Temple returned to the house to find Doc Kildenning administering a dose of morphine to the injured man. Malloy's eyes were open, fever-bright, but lucid; when he spoke it was in clear accents.

"Not sure how much sand I got left, Buck," Genesee Malloy said. "Lots of things to say to you. I got to let you know how wrong I been about my daughter's choice of a man."

Temple crouched at the bedside, flicking a glance toward the doctor, and getting Kildenning's permissive nod.

"You get some sleep before you start worrying over anything, Genesee. You owe me nothing."

The injured man rolled his head feebly on the pillow. He glanced around the room to make sure his daughter was not present, then turned his eyes on Buck Temple.

"What I got to say I don't specially want Avis to hear, son," came the oldster's dull whisper. "Like Jord Ramont sending a flunky to Walla Walla to tally you the night you left the pen, remember? I knew about that deal and did nothing to prevent it. I guess greed for power and money makes a man into a criminal perty easy, Buck."

Temple made no answer; it struck him as strange that he found it impossible to harbor any malice for this man, here at the end.

"I wasn't on that raid above the High Rim yesterday," Malloy went on, "but I knew where Ramont and Corson and the others were riding and what they aimed to do. I'll spend my hitch in hell repenting all I could have done, but didn't."

The old man's fingers plucked at the blanket which covered his paralyzed limbs.

"Speaking of Corson," Malloy said, "it was him that shot you the day you rescued Ramont from Brockway's stage, Buck. It was Corson who murdered old Bill Winn and dropped the sheriff. That's why I'm glad old Si Larbuck cashed in Corson's chips yesterday."

Temple remained wholly silent, knowing Malloy had to have his chance to clear his soul.

"The whole rotten deal—I was a silent pardner in it from the first," Malloy went on. "Ramont paying Vance Bluedom to bushwhack McAllister and bribing Karl Gothe to lay the blame on you. A word from me at the trial could have kept you from going to Walla Walla last fall, Buck. It's hell to be dying with so many blots on my book."

Avis came into the room then, bearing a green tin box. She placed it on the bed beside her father and knelt down beside Buck Temple, slipping her hand in his.

"I'm deeding Broken Bit back to you," Genesee went on, his voice beginning to wander as the morphine took its sedative hold on his nerve centers. "For what it's worth, I'm restoring your old homeplace to you, Buck."

Something akin to embarrassment needled Temple as he saw Avis, obeying Genesee's whispered instructions, hand him a legal paper from the tin box, and put an indelible pencil between her father's fingers.

He turned aside, watching Doc Kildenning sort out his surgical instruments on a boiled towel at the nearby dresser that had belonged to Buck's mother. He had no desire to watch Genesee Malloy affix his signature to the quit-claim deed; he felt no triumph at realizing that Broken Bit was his again.

Temple moved over to stand by Doc Kildenning.

"How long you figure he's got?"

Kildenning's face was professionally inscrutable.

"I'd say twenty years."

"He won't die?"

"Not of his broken vertebrae. But Genesee will never walk again, Buck. He will be paralyzed for the rest of his time. For Avis's sake, it's too bad you didn't find him dead at the top of that tree."

Temple shuddered, knowing that old Genesee would infinitely have preferred death to lifelong invalidism. He turned to see that the man on the bed had slipped into a drug-induced coma. Avis was sobbing silently at the bedside, her head buried in the crook of her father's arm, the Broken Bit deed clutched in her other hand.

Leaving the house, Temple made his way out to rejoin Mary Wunderling at the hammock. He reported briefly, "Genesee's paralyzed for life. He just did the penance of deeding this ranch back to me."

The girl swung her legs to the ground and looked up at Temple.

"That evil old man has done you no favor, Buck. He knows that your Broken Bit is ruined."

Temple nodded. "Yes. It was a gesture of restitution on Genesee's part. He thought he was dying."

Temple saw the girl hesitate, searching for words to express something that was sorely troubling her.

"Buck, I could have killed Ramont back there," she said, finally. "I've bagged many a deer at a thousand yards in worse light. But when I found a man lined up in my sights, I failed you, Buck."

He grinned softly. "No, Mary. I'm glad you didn't. It is not a pleasant thing to live with, knowing you have killed a man."

She came to her feet, smoothing her doeskin skirt.

"Are we riding back to Rimrock now?"

"Not just yet, Mary. I've got to stick around on the off-chance that Ramont does come back tonight. He undoubtedly has valuables in his safe that he'd want to take with him."

The girl laid a hand on his arm.

"If he does return to Broken Bit, you know you'll have to kill him?"

"Yes. There's no other answer to that, Mary."

Chapter 19

Soot-blackened fire fighters began to drift back to the Broken Bit ranch house as sundown burned out beyond the smoke pall which obscured the Cascades' snow-crusted skyline.

Out from Rimrock came a hayrick driven by Sheriff Canuck Brockway, making his first trip out of the county seat since the Grapevine Curve ambush; his wagon was loaded with Rimrock womenfolk and supplies of food for the wearied fire fighters.

It was a polygot crowd which gathered in the Broken Bit yard, illumined by lanterns hanging from the box elders.

Jord Ramont's lumberjacks were here, bull-chested men with hobbed lace boots and ash-grimed logging shirts. Men alien to this cattleland, aware of its brooding hostility; they kept together in a tight group, feeling lost without the presence of their employer.

In equal number were the ranch owners and their cowhands, gathered here to fight the common enemy of the fire, but remembering now the more sinister purpose that had caused them to rendezvous at Overmile's Box O the night before.

Rounding out this scene were the fifty-odd fire fighters recruited by Buck Temple in Rimrock—

butchers and bartenders, storekeepers and courthouse clerks, gamblers and stable hostlers— the high and the humble of the cow town's populace.

Sheriff Brockway remained on the seat of the big grub wagon which became the focal point of this milling, low-talking, somehow subdued mass of humanity. His star gleamed conspicuously in the lantern shine; his crutches were tilted against the footboard, the only evidence that he was not his old self.

Aunt Molly Brockway was superintending the womenfolk, who included in their number Straight-Edge Josie and her social outcasts from the county's only brothel. These women passed from group to group with steaming buckets of coffee and trays of sandwiches and pickles and doughnuts.

This night, the occasion should have been in the nature of a triumphant celebration, by reason of their victory over the red menace which had threatened the futures of every soul present. But it was not; Buck Temple, moving here and there around the yard, read in the tense attitudes of these weary men a tacit waiting for hell to break loose.

The meal was finished and there was talk among the townspeople of getting back to their homes when Buck Temple threaded his big roan saddler across the yard.

He reined up alongside the sheriff's grub wagon, waiting for the crowd to hear what he had to say.

Three component factions were here: the loggers and lumber freighters keeping together close by the ranch house porch; the cattlemen lining the outside fence with grizzled old Texas Sam Waterby, swathed in bandages, fronting them; the Rimrock citizens finding places out under the box elders, sensing that high drama was about to be enacted here.

Buck Temple was the core of this meeting; every eye was on him as he swung his roan to face the lumbermen.

"Where—" He broke off, turning to face Sheriff Brockway, "I'd as soon you weren't here, Canuck."

His old friend reached up to unpin his law badge.

"This is your hour, Buck," the old Canadian said. "You call the dances the way you see fit."

Brockway had spoken in the softest of voices; but like a rock dropped in a deep pool, the eddying ripples of the sheriff's resignation from office spread to the far fringes of the crowd.

Temple turned his attention back to the grim-faced, sullenly waiting crew of loggers and wagoneers.

"Where is Jord Ramont?"

No answer was immediately forthcoming

from Ramont's henchmen. Finally a high-line rigger who served as logging foreman spoke up hoarsely, "Don't ask us, mister. We ain't seen hide nor hair of Ramont since after the fire busted out."

Hoofs stirred across the trampled lawn as Tex Waterby and his forty-odd neighbors moved away from the fence, forming a solid phalanx backing up Buck Temple.

"Right this minute," Temple went on, "we are looking at twenty-odd loggers who stampeded our beef over the High Rim yesterday morning. We realize we can't pick you out and condemn you in any court of law. That is why this thing is going to be settled now, here, tonight, by our own means."

Temple's ringing words brought a rasping of gun metal leaving scabbards from the close ranks of the cowmen massed behind him. Temple went on quickly, staving off any premature break.

"You men know that Ramont has lost his lumber contract with Pacific & Western?"

The loggers' spokesman answered sullenly, "We know that. But Ramont aims to keep loggin' up in the government timber. There's a big market for lumber in this territory."

Buck Temple smiled grimly. "Your only right of way to the government lands is through Glacier Canyon. It so happens that Genesee Malloy has deeded Broken Bit back to me. I am closing Broken Bit and Glacier Canyon to your equipment as of tonight."

Temple's words brought a tumult of applause from the mounted cattlemen and the Rimrock citizenry across the yard—it was their first intimation of Malloy's action in restoring Broken Bit to its former owner.

When quiet was restored, Ramont's logging boss countered angrily, "We got another right o' way rigged up, mister. Jord Ramont's got a deal on with Hal Dikus for timber rights in Goose Creek Canyon. We don't need Glacier."

A rider spurred out of the line of horsemen behind Buck Temple and reined up at the latter's stirrup. Glancing around, Buck recognized the soot-grimed figure of the Lazy D boss, Hal Dikus.

"I've been courtin' Jord Ramont's favor all along, Ellerby," Dikus addressed the lumbermen's spokesman, "but the time comes when a man sees the error of his ways, I reckon. Fightin' that fire today, seein' Buck Temple here risk his hide to save old Malloy's bacon, I did some powerful thinkin'. Buck Temple's been fightin' a one-man battle for us ranchers, savin' our range for greedy hawgs like myself. Nope, Ellerby, my deal with Jord Ramont ain't reached the paper signin' stage. Lazy D is closed to anything connected with loggin'."

Buck Temple put his grateful smile on old Hal

Dikus; across the yard he saw Mary Wunderling watching him, and caught her signal of congratulations.

When the pandemonium following Dikus' pledge of loyalty to his own breed had died away, Temple turned back to Ellerby.

"This country is closed to loggers from here on out," he said quietly. "I have but to say the word, Ellerby, and these cattlemen behind me will move in with hot lead and hang rope. You are on my land. Here and now, I'm ordering you off it. Any logger who lets tomorrow's sunrise catch him anywhere on Broken Bit will get himself lynched."

Buck Temple had given his ultimatum; he had the guns to back his orders. No longer was he fighting a lone battle; the men and women who made this cattle country were sitting in judgment here tonight, backing Temple to the last notch.

Ellerby stepped away from the ranks of loggers, sweat beads glistening on his hairy face as he took the measure of the waiting cowmen ringing his partisans with leveled guns. He saw nervous fingers fiddling with coiled lariats, and knew the sinister meaning behind those moves. Forty triggers were being held in leash solely by Buck Temple's personality; this was an explosive moment where a wrong word could bring bloody slaughter to Broken Bit.

"We'll head outside on Ramont's wagons

tonight, mister," the woodsman voiced his surrender. "Call off your dawgs. We know when we're licked. There ain't one of us who cottons to the idea of fightin' for a man who's skipped out and left us to face the music."

Temple wheeled his horse around, his eyes seeking out old Tex Waterby of the Diamond X outfit.

"Men, this ends it. Get back to your spreads. We've all got work to do before the big outfits down below start hazin' their herds up here for summer graze."

A great collective sigh of pent-up breath sounded in the utter silence then, from the loggers as well as the Rimrock settlers. Every soul here realized that in this moment, peace had returned to the east slope of the Cascades; that this feud had burned itself out with the same violent finality as the forest fire these men of many divergent interests had joined to fight this day.

These cattlemen had lost the bulk of their own beef, but there was still the dependable revenue to be gained from the leasing of their summer graze to the cattle syndicates from the arid prairies of Ellensburg and Yakima.

On that foundation would the foothill ranches rebuild their fortunes. The slaughter up at the High Rim became, therefore, a transient thing, a setback which the country could take in its stride.

Doc Kildenning began the exodus away from Broken Bit, with Avis Malloy sitting on the seat of the buckboard beside him, her injured father resting on piled-up mattresses in the wagon box.

Mary Wunderling and Buck Temple left the ranch together. Reaching Rimrock, the girl accepted Aunt Molly Brockway's invitation to rest up at the sheriff's home, while Buck once more sought the sanctuary of the doctor's stable.

Throughout the remainder of this historic night, Arrowhead Creek's wagon road rumbled with wagon traffic as Jord Ramont's big Conestogas pulled out of Broken Bit, loaded with loggers and their bedding instead of fresh-sawed lumber.

Midafternoon of the following day found Buck Temple and Doc Kildenning making old Si Larbuck comfortable on a pile of hay in the back of a borrowed democrat wagon. With Mary Wunderling and Buck in the driver's seat and their saddle horses trailing behind, they headed down Coppertooth Pass toward the girl's homestead.

They found Jingo Paloo waiting for them at Mary's cabin, back from his weekly tour of the mailboxes up and down the foothill circuit. Si Larbuck was transferred from the wagon to the same bed where Buck had recovered from his wounds.

Later, watching the long blue shadow of Coppertooth Peak creep across the grassy flats of

Mary's homestead park, Buck and Paloo squatted on the stone doorstep and sought comfort in their tobacco while Mary busied herself cooking supper.

To eastward, beyond the foothills where the vast desert had its beginning, a smudge of alkali dust had formed its smoke-like mass over the Cascade spurs; and both men saw in that dust the answer to the Rimrock ranchers' prayers.

The cloven hoofs of thousands of Yakima steers had stirred up that smudge. Beef herds being hazed up from the drought-stricken fringe of the desert bordering the Columbia, making their annual trek to the lush summer graze under the High Rim, which Buck Temple's crusade had made secure.

"Well, it's been a long pull," Jingo commented, watching the first stars break through the arching heavens. "Where do you go from here, Buck?"

Temple stirred his long legs, rubbing the worn spot on his chap flank where his gun holster had had its place.

"Waterby's offered me a ramrod's job on Diamond X."

Paloo plucked a grass stem and started nibbling it. "I wonder," the Texan drawled thoughtfully, "where Jord Ramont hightailed to. I'd like to think that fire trapped him up there."

Temple shrugged. "I doubt it. Ramont realized

his string was frayed out; that's why he tried to kill me at the end. I reckon we won't see his shadow around the Rimrock country again."

They heard Mary's welcome dinner call, and went to the back porch to wash up. Temple was toweling his face when he caught sight of the blinking flashes of Captain Collie's signal lantern far up the Pass.

He was about to call Mary out of the house to transcribe the message when he saw the girl was already watching from her kitchen window.

At his elbow, Jingo Paloo was mumbling: "T—O—W—N. Town. W—A—I—T."

Paloo lost track and Temple grinned. "You never told me you savvied Morse code, Jingo. What's the dirt Collie is dishing out now?"

"Mary taught me how to—"

From the window of the kitchen Mary Wunderling called sharply, interrupting Paloo, "Collie just wants to know how Si Larbuck is making out after his wagon ride down the Pass. I imagine Doc Kildenning is behind that."

Temple saw Paloo's stare follow the girl outside. She had a lighted lamp in her hand and, using a skillet for a shutter, flashed answering dots and dashes back to the old army veteran at his station fifteen miles away.

"I told him Si's in fine shape," Mary explained, when Collie's brief acknowledgment flickered back to them, like the pulsations of a remote planet. "Come on in and eat before the soup gets cold, you two."

Seated at the same table with Jingo Paloo, with Mary in the other room arranging Si Larbuck's supper dishes, Buck Temple suddenly pushed his plate back.

"Not hungry," he said to the mail carrier, and passed Mary on her way back from Larbuck's bedroom.

For some reason, Buck Temple found himself feeling out of place, unwanted as long as Jingo Paloo was also a guest of Mary Wunderling's. He had a feeling of not belonging here, of being an interloper; and that unrest was still riding him when, a few minutes later, Jingo Paloo strode out the front door alongside which Temple was hunkered down, smoking.

Paloo ignored Temple's presence there, heading out toward the barn.

Struck by a sense that something was amiss, Buck Temple flicked his cigarette aside and stepped indoors. Mary Wunderling was standing before the table, a stricken look on her face; it was a moment before Temple's presence broke through.

"Mary, you and Jingo ain't had a tiff?"

Suddenly, unaccountably, Mary Wunderling turned away and he saw sobs break the firm angles of her shoulders.

"No tiff, Buck," she whispered. "Jingo is not

the man. I—I just had to tell him so. It was hard to do. I like him so much."

He stepped forward as she turned; her love for him was shining in her eyes, beyond mistaking. The full ripeness of her slightly parted lips was an invitation no longer to be resisted; it went beyond the bounds of loyalty for a friend, it was something that had to come out of him before it destroyed his peace of mind for all time to be.

He pulled her hard against him, nestling her glossy chestnut head under the hard angle of his jaw; and he found himself whispering, "I broke it off final with Avis yesterday, Mary, there in front of Gothe's store."

They moved apart, then let their lips meet crushingly in the first kiss they had shared. All the old wants and hungers of Temple's lonely heart surfaced in the white heat of this newfound ecstasy, and he knew that Mary Wunderling was his and his alone, and that it would never be other than this.

"I have loved you for so long, Buck Temple," the girl was saying, the hard pounding of her heart tight against his. "Long before I found you in that snowbank, I guess. I have loved you with a little child's faith, and with the last corner of my soul."

He rocked her in his arms, talking to her as if she had been a little child seeking his arms for cherished comfort. She said, "This homestead is ours to share, Buck. It will make up your loss of Broken Bit. It will be my dowry."

He heard himself musing, "What was that brand you had figgered out, Mary?"

"A caduceus. The Army's Medical Corps insignia. It's a sentimental thing to do, Buck. For Dad's sake—"

"The boys'll call it Snake on a Stick, sure as—"

"It will be our ranch, Buck. Our home to pass onto our children. That's why I clung to this homestead after what happened. I knew some-how someday you would come riding "

The thud of Jingo Paloo's boots outside jerked Buck Temple back to stern reality, reminding him of the unhappy duty that he had in breaking this news to his friend who loved Mary no less passionately for having lost her.

Mary broke out of Temple's embrace and ran to the door. Her tragic voice floated back to Temple as he stood by the table. "You're going in his stead, Jingo? No—"

A harsh thought wiped out the happiness that had settled on Temple's mouth. He strode quickly out of doors, to find Mary clinging to the Texan's arms as he stood hooking a stirrup over his saddle horn, preparatory to adjusting his latigo.

"How else can it be, Mary?" Paloo ground out. "This thing has got to be s—"

Temple loomed in the moonlight beside this pair.

"I want to see Jingo alone, Mary."

The girl reached up to pull Jingo Paloo's head down, kissing him on the mouth; and then, with a sharp intake of breath, she ran back into the cabin.

"Jingo," Temple began, "I—"

The Texan's bleak grin silenced him. "I know, kid. It's been written on Mary's face for a long time. For her, it's always been you. I'll git over it, knowing it was you."

Temple gripped his old friend's hand, his throat suddenly too constricted for speech.

Paloo jerked his cinch tight and unhooked his stirrup. He twisted his face into a false grin.

"Well, amigo, I got to shag along," he said briskly. "The U. S. mail don't wait for hell or high water, let alone busted hearts. Besides, you two got a lot to—"

Temple wrenched the reins out of Paloo's hand.

"Jingo, what was that code message of Collie's?"

Paloo ducked his head, searching his vest pocket for the makings, patently stalling for time.

"Why," Paloo laughed with forced casualness, "Mary told you. Doc was wondering how Larbuck—"

"Don't lie to me, Jingo."

Paloo let his arms drop by his sides, the unfired cigarette spilling from his lips. All expression was rubbed off his puckish, homely face as he

265

lifted his eyes to meet the imperative strike of Temple's gaze.

"I guess a man has to do his own fightin'," Paloo mumbled, "but I could have handled this okay, like I did that bushwhacker over in Walla Walla. I got less to lose."

"Jingo, damn you, stop beating around the bush."

Paloo sucked in a deep breath.

"Well, Jord Ramont's waitin' for you up at Rimrock," the Texan blurted. "Waitin' for you to show up and settle your affairs with gunplay. Now you satisfied?"

Temple nodded, as if he had been sure of what Paloo was going to tell him. Something like relief touched the big rider's eyes, calming the torment there.

"I can make it to town inside of two hours. Don't let Mary know I've gone until I'm well on my way, if you can."

"Buck, let me ride along."

Temple was already heading for the corral to saddle up. "No. I want to borrow your gun, Jingo. Mary's doesn't balance right."

Chapter 20

A full moon was at Buck Temple's back when he emerged from Arrowhead Creek Canyon at the outskirts of Rimrock. He had chosen to follow the creek from Mary Wunderling's homestead, knowing the risk of ambush if he traveled the stage road up Coppertooth Pass.

Main Street's shade trees threw their dappled shadows along the silver dust between the battlemented rows of false fronts. As Temple's approach was telegraphed to the town by the hollow drumming of the blue roan's hoofs, he took notice that the streets appeared sinister and totally deserted.

He thought, the town knows I've come to settle this with Ramont tonight. And he dropped a hand to loosen the rubber-stocked Navy six gun in his holster, the Colt Jingo Paloo had loaned him for this showdown.

Passing the courthouse, Temple saw the pink coal of a cigar ebbing and glowing in the murky doorway of the jail office, and knew that Canuck Brockway had stationed himself at this vantage point commanding a view of the street's length.

"Damn old Collie's meddling hide," came the sheriff's voice. "Damn these crutches that keep me from attending to this business myself."

Temple reined up briefly, the moonlight limning the edges of his tall shape in the saddle.

"You've turned your star over to Mose Hartley. Remember?"

The red eye of Brockway's cigar butt described the fiery path of the old Canadian's gesture upstreet. His words ran softly through the mealy night toward the Rimrock rider:

"Watch your back, son. Hartley's gone up to the Rim with a wagon to bring back those dead ones. You're on your own. Luck."

Temple touched Blue's flanks with rowels, his eyes watching the shadowed galleries of the deadfalls and honkytonks on either side of the street with a wary thoroughness. Brockway didn't know where Jord Ramont was lurking; if he had he would have divulged that vital information to Temple.

A lone man crossed the street in front of Temple, heading into the Trail House. It was Doc Kildenning with his black satchel, paying a visit to Genesee Malloy.

Captain Collie spoke from the inky blackness of Karl Gothe's trading post porch when Temple came abreast of him.

"He's up in his room oilin' his guns, Buck. Mary said you'd pulled out for Diamond X. Knew she was lyin'. Knowed you'd show up. Told that bastard as much."

Buck Temple dismounted, flexing his fingers,

268

his gaze fixed on the lamplight's glow showing through pinholes in the shade drawn over Jord Ramont's window in the hotel.

He hitched Blue to the Mile-High Mercantile rack. As he did so, Temple saw the distorted shadow of Jord Ramont blot across the window shade like something cut out of black wood. Buck was stepping away from his horse when Ramont ran up the shade and leaned out the open window, staring down the street toward the Pass.

Ramont was a prime target, etched there against the yellow lamp glow of the hotel room. But Temple's six gun was still in holster as he sent his low challenge winging toward Ramont.

"Over here, Jord. You want me to come up after you?"

The lumber boss jerked his head around, seeking the source of that voice; Ramont spotted Buck Temple standing in front of Gothe's boarded-up store, hands hanging loose at his sides, legs widespread in a tense attitude of waiting.

A sepulchral silence congealed Rimrock as men standing in darkened doorways and behind unlighted saloon windows up and down the street waited for Jord Ramont's reaction.

"By God, stay where you are!" Ramont's bull voice echoed off the false fronts. "It's me that's coming out to smoke you to hell, Temple, like

I promised you a long time back. You stand hitched."

Temple's head tipped. "I'm waiting," he said.

Ramont withdrew from the window; the lamp flame jarred to the slam of his bedroom door.

Seconds grew into a minute; the eyes of the town were riveted to the screen door of the Trail House lobby, waiting for Jord Ramont to get downstairs.

A man somewhere off to Temple's left warned in a low voice, "Keep a stirrup eye peeled on the fire escape, Buck."

Timed with that voice, a stab of bore-flame cut the stygian gut of the alley alongside Trail House; the bullet's air whip was a tangible thrust against Buck Temple's head as he turned to duck into the concealing blackness under the wooden awning of Gothe's store.

Palming the Navy .45, Temple laid two fast shots into the maw of that alley, knowing that Ramont had left the hotel by the fire escape ladder. He heard his bullets slap the corner clapboards of Trail House, followed by a quick shuffle of boots as Jord Ramont shifted position.

A dog started barking, to set up clamorous echoes along the street; a man cursed from a livery stable's door, knowing Temple's acute need for absolute quiet if he were to gauge Ramont's movements through the far shadows.

Another gunshot broke through the dog's

barking, coming this time from the front center of the saddle shop next door to the hotel. This time it was a rifle; the steel-jacketed bullet thunked into Karl Gothe's warped signboard directly above Temple's head.

"Come out where a man can see you, damn it!" Jord Ramont bawled with berserk anger.

Temple heard Captain Collie's asthmatic breathing somewhere behind him on the porch. His eyes plumbed the gray wall of the saddle shop, obscured now by dust stirred up by a running dog, and a bursting impatience needled him into betraying his own position with an answering yell.

"Same applies to you, Ramont. Get out in the open."

Temple caught sight of Ramont then, running in a stooped-over position up the street. The same voice that had warned Temple a moment ago cut the gelid silence of the moonlit scene.

"Jord's packing a carbeen, Buck, and aiming to get out of range of that pistol of yours. Want me to toss you a .30-30?"

At that moment Jord Ramont left the shadowed side of the street and walked into full view of the town, sixty yards away and halting in the dead center of the street. The lumber boss carried a short-barreled Remington-Keen rifle at hip level; the moon's rays showed the level searching of that .45-70's muzzle.

Temple's thumb eared the knurled hammer of the Colt to full cock, calculating the range with an expert detachment. Satisfied with his judgment, the big Broken Bit cowman came out of the concealment of Gothe's porch, his shadow waggling across the wheel ruts of the street as he stalked toward Ramont at a quartering angle, Colt muzzle tipped skyward.

The hidden onlookers on both sides of the street muttered their alarm as they saw Ramont whip rifle stock to cheek and drop to one knee. They saw the lumberman's first shot kick dirt against the batwings of Temple's chaps, saw the cowpuncher make a quick zigzagging leap.

Ramont was emptying his rifle's magazine now as fast as he could trigger the Remington-Keen. Such shooting was inevitably wild, and Temple kept weaving up the street, mentally counting Ramont's shots.

He concluded Ramont's eight-load magazine was empty before his ears caught the click of the firing pin in an empty breech; and his gun dropped level as he saw Ramont hurl the useless rifle to one side, his hand instantly filled with the Root sidehammer .36 he carried in an armpit holster.

Temple called out, "I got no particular stomach for killing you, Ramont. Get your arms up and I'll take you down to Brockway to stand legal trial."

Ramont tilted back his head and gave vent to a maniac's screeching laugh. His logger's shirt was a blood-red target there in the moonglow; he had braced his booted feet wide, waiting and watching as Temple's inexorable pace cut down the gap between them.

"You cut a wide splash around these hills, Temple." Ramont's jeer filled the canyon of false fronts with sound. "I chose to make it this way to show this town the size of your yellow streak."

With less than forty feet between them, Buck Temple halted. With that corner of his brain that was not concentrating on this grim game, he heard Avis Malloy calling both their names from an upper window of Trail House, behind him. But his every instinct was channeled into a tight track now, every nerve fined down as the run of seconds brought this climatic showdown into sharpening focus.

Temple's agate eyes were watching the big sidehammer Colt in Ramont's fist, hugged to his hip now.

"Ramont," Temple spoke again, "drop your gun. I don't—"

The lumberman jerked trigger even as he swiveled his big body and started racing for the black archway of a livery stable off to his right, shooting as he ran.

Temple heard the whistling passage of lead bracketing him; his own gun started heating up echoes, the Navy's muzzle swiveling to follow Ramont's low-crouched race toward the barn's shelter.

Yards short of the livery stable's shadow, Ramont broke stride and fell heavily on the moonlit dust. The town, watching from its collective doors and windows, saw Ramont come to his feet, fighting the dead weight of his .36 as Temple continued to drive in his shots with relentless precision.

The gruesome slam and thud of that lead drilling human flesh and bone was clearly audible to the crouched audience inside the livery stable. It seemed impossible that Jord Ramont could take that hammering and still be on his feet.

With one cartridge left in his .45 cylinder, Buck Temple stopped shooting, tipping his smoking Colt upward.

He kept his breath tight-held during the span of time it took Ramont's sidehammer Colt to slip from his lax fingers and hit the dirt. Then the lumber boss' knees unhinged and he pitched in a twisting sidewise motion to measure his length on the hoof-trampled ground.

A crawling puddle of blood took form under Ramont's head, reflecting the moon in ruby glints. A cowboy moved cautiously out of the livery's doorway and prodded that limp shape with a boot toe. His ghastly whisper reached Temple:

"He's dead."

Gunpowder's raw stench was in Temple's nostrils. He thrust Jingo Paloo's hot-barreled gun under his belt and turned slowly to walk back toward his saddle horse.

Rimrock came alive at last. Men broke out of buildings up and down the street, clamoring hoarsely, running toward the bullet-riddled corpse in front of the stable.

Reaching his horse, Buck Temple saw Avis Malloy crossing toward him from the Trail House. Her face was a stark, chalky mask in the moonlight as she flung her arms around his chest and broke into uncontrolled sobbing against him.

"I died a thousand times watching you stalk Jord." The girl finally became rational again. "We can make a clean start of it from here, Buck. Please—"

Temple disengaged the girl's hands from his shirt, his face inflexibly set.

"Avis, what would you be telling Ramont if that were me lying there instead?"

The girl's face went soft, ugly in its tragedy, her wet cheeks sagging.

"Buck, you can't have stopped loving me. Such a short, short time ago you even saved Jord's life for my sake."

Temple shook his head.

"Avis, haven't you ever wondered what made the sheriff suddenly drop his charges against me?

Haven't you wondered what could have made him cancel that bounty?"

"No—no, Buck."

"Then I'll tell you, and let you draw your own conclusions. I didn't save Ramont for your sake. I saved him to keep him from hanging for a killing I committed the night I walked up from Si Larbuck's with the idea of seeing you, Avis. At that, getting shot by Karl Gothe would have been easier to take than finding you in Ramont's arms."

Captain Collie, his tarnished epaulets catching the moon's gleaming, sidled out of the shadow to interrupt these two.

"Want I should signal down to Mary how it turned out, Buck?" the old drunkard asked. "She'll be anxious to know."

Avis Malloy saw Buck turn to his horse, and knew by that act that he was banishing her forever from his life. She heard him speak to Collie, as if from a great distance.

"I wish you would, Cap. Tell her I'm on my way home."

Standing there in the street's dust, Avis Malloy watched the Broken Bit waddy put his blue roan down the street. She saw him lift his hat to Canuck Brockway as he passed the jail; he was riding at full gallop when he crossed the Arrowhead Creek bridge.

Avis thought of her invalided father, her

unshakeable responsibility through all the empty years that stretched ahead. There was no solace for her in the knowledge that her destiny would have been no different if Jord Ramont had walked away from this gun fight tonight.

Through swimming eyes, Avis Malloy stared down the gulf of Coppertooth Pass, watching the dust of Temple's departure settle in the moonlight. Beyond the hard angles of the cow town's buildings she saw the familiar loom of the Peak, and the low-hung star caught in the shadows at its base, marking the windows of Mary Wunderling's remote cabin.

That lighted window was a beacon guiding Buck Temple down the mountain, away from her arms, lost to her beyond any hope of recall. This was the harvest of her father's ambitions, the retribution for her own selfish connivings. Mary Wunderling's light was the lodestar of love and hope that was calling Buck Temple home.

Turning, Avis Malloy made her way across the street to the Trail House and her waiting father.

Center Point Large Print
600 Brooks Road / PO Box 1
Thorndike, ME 04986-0001 USA

(207) 568-3717

US & Canada:
1 800 929-9108
www.centerpointlargeprint.com